We Were Not Like Other People

We Were Not Like Other People

Other People

Ephraim Sevela

translated by Antonina W. Bouis

HARPER & ROW, PUBLISHERS   NEW YORK
Grand Rapids, Philadelphia, St. Louis, San Francisco,
London, Singapore, Sydney, Tokyo, Toronto

Typography by Joyce Hopkins
1 2 3 4 5 6 7 8 9 10
First Edition

Library of Congress Cataloging-in-Publication Data
Sevela, Éfraim.
    We were not like other people / by Ephraim Sevela : translated by
Antonina Bouis. — 1st ed.
        p.   cm.
    Translated from the Russian.
    Summary: Separated from his family when the Germans invade Russia
during World War II, a young boy learns to fend for himself and earn
a living whenever and however he can.
    ISBN 0-06-025507-2 $. — ISBN 0-06-025508-0 (lib. bdg.) : $
    1. Sevela, Éfraim—Juvenile fiction.   2. Jews—Soviet Union—
Juvenile fiction.   3 World War, 1939–1945—Soviet Union—Juvenile
fiction.   [1. Sevela, Éfraim—Fiction.   2. World War, 1939–1945—
Soviet Union—Fiction.   3. Jews—Soviet Union—Fiction.]
I. Title.
PZ7.S514We 1989   89-11015
[Fic]—dc20   CIP
                                                              AC

To the memory of my mother,
who did not survive her separation from me

We Were Not Like Other People

Prelude

I remember a bright sunny winter day in the Urals. The frosts had broken. There was a hint of distant spring in the air. The village, drowned in deep drifts, sent up soft, steamy puffs of smoke from its chimneys. The snow no longer squeaked underfoot, but cracked juicily as it settled.

It was a day of rest. We poured out into the street from the dormitory of the vocational school. The sun was blinding, and we squinted as if we had just come out from a dark cellar.

We were hungry, and we were children. So we held the grainy melting snow in our hands and licked it, bit it, the way once upon a time, before the war, we ate ice cream.

On the bare branches of birches, crows called to one another. Teasing them, we shouted in reply, and our merry chatter enlivened the street with its houses almost roof deep in snow. The nearby mountains, which surrounded the small factory town with granite cliffs, echoed our cries.

Our street ended in a square covered with snow, and in the center a wooden obelisk rose from the snow—a monument to local partisans who died in the Civil War, long before we were born. We liked that monument. Wide wooden steps led up to it, and we sat on them, in the sunshine, forming a circle and gambling with homemade cards. In lieu of money we bet sticky and sour pieces of black bread from our rations.

The obelisk's pyramid was faced on four sides with gray, time-cracked planks, and large letters carved out of wood were nailed to the planks. They said:

> Walk without fear on dead bodies.
> Carry their banner forward.
> The dead don't need anthems or tears;
> Give them their due respect.

Some of the letters had cracked and fallen off, leaving rusty nailheads and a faded outline. The remaining ones were puffed up like little old men under snowy caps and with beards of icicles.

We adored that poem. We agreed that the dead didn't need anthems or tears. And the call to walk on dead bodies gave us a thrilling chill. I couldn't imagine how you walk on dead bodies without fear.

I had seen more than one dead person. We had our corpses at school. Little ones. They were buried in children's coffins that looked like toys. They were boys and girls like me, but they couldn't take the hunger and the hard work.

Death awaited us at the factory. It hid in the spinning metal parts, in the fists of the lathes.

We worked standing on platforms—pine blocks—so that we could reach the levers. Our hunger made us dizzy—the weaker ones passed out. If they were lucky, they fell backward. They quickly revived after the fall on the stone floor, and after catching their breath, they could climb up and turn off the machine.

But if they fell forward? No one ever fell forward and lived. They fell onto machinery that immediately rolled up their shirts, turned them upside down, and smashed them into a cast-iron frame. You couldn't even hear the cracking ribs above the factory din.

Reading the poem on the obelisk, I thought that I wasn't big enough yet to walk on dead bodies. And then came an opportunity to prove that I was fearless, that I was a man.

We were playing cards on the sun-warmed dry steps of the obelisk, and a kid with a short wet nose and sunken blue cheeks, from the metal-working shop, whined like a puppy.

"Come on, guys! Chop off my hand! Just a piece, come on . . ."

"Get out of here!" we barked. "Chop your own hand off."

In one hand he held a chunk of rock and in the other a piece of steel sharpened on one edge till it shone. He had sharpened it in his shop.

"How can I chop it off myself?" he whined. "I don't

have enough hands for that. I need two to chop—one for the rock and one for the knife."

"Then get out of here!"

"Bastards," he said. "You won't help a guy out. I'm gonna die in that shop . . . but if I'm hurt, I'll get a month in the hospital to rest up."

He came up to each of us in turn holding out the rock and the homemade knife. The boys looked away.

"Bitches! Devils!" he swore. "How hard is it to help out a comrade? One hit and that's it! And I'm saved. I won't die. Where's your conscience? I'm asking you to be human."

I glanced over at him: He was asking for someone to cripple his hand in the same way starving people beg for food. And my pals who were just like him, hungry and mean, laughed and sent him away.

He stopped in front of me. Our eyes met. I didn't look away.

"Will you do it?" Hope shone in his eyes. Hope and fear. He realized that this was it. Another minute or so and blood would spurt from his smashed hand. He was afraid.

"You'll do it?" he repeated softly.

"If you want, I will," I said coldly.

He handed me the rough stone and the cold piece of razor-sharp steel.

I looked into his eyes again.

"You haven't changed your mind? It's not too late."

"No, no . . . chop!"

He went up on the top step right by the obelisk and sat down, his back against it. First he put down his right hand on the step, but he changed his mind and placed his left hand palm down, pressing so hard it was flat.

"That piece . . . there," he said pointing to the tensed muscle below his pinky. The pinky twitched and so did the other fingers. The muscle that was about to be chopped off grew white, as if the blood had rushed off to escape.

He took the piece of steel from me and placed the blade at the base of the muscle. All I had to do was hit it from above with the rock.

I raised my hand with the rock.

The black coats, playing cards nearby, froze and stared tensely at him and at me.

"You haven't changed your mind?" I asked, feeling my hand start to tremble.

"Chop, I said!"

He moved the blade slightly, making the doomed piece smaller.

I thought that for him the most important thing was to damage his hand and spend time in the hospital. Naturally he was afraid, but clearly he was malnourished and only hospitalization would save him. And he wouldn't get into a hospital without bodily damage.

"This is the last time I'm asking," I whispered.

"Just chop!" he shouted.

I lowered the rock.

Like a slice of sausage the cut muscle fell off, revealing pale-pink flesh. It fell on the step below, plopped on the wood, and lay there. Not a drop of blood.

I sharply looked at the hand. Two streams of blood throbbed like tiny fountains from two arteries opened by the blade. He clutched his left hand in his right, but the blood seeped through his fingers and fell in thick drops, immediately absorbed by the wood.

Our eyes met once again. His lips were trembling. And I saw hatred in his eyes.

"You bastard!" he hissed through clenched teeth.

"You asked me to. I wanted to help. . . ."

But he ran off, doubled over, to the dorm.

"He asked me," I said, turning for support to my friends who stood on the sidelines. I didn't find any sympathy. One after the other they turned their backs to me.

I then swore that I would remain an observer in such situations. Like my comrades, I would give only sympathy, and not take on a sin, even for salvation.

A little over a year later I was confronted by a choice again. I was in the army then. Our front was attacking, pressing the German divisions into an enormous ring on the Berezina River. The Germans were trying to break through, and they concentrated a fist in a narrow sector and punched—right where our regiment was. We suffered terrible losses. More than half our troops were killed, and the survivors, deafened and stunned, ran under steady fire from the German artillery.

I was getting out with my friend Samokhin. We ran along potato fields plowed up by shells. Unripe tubers showed pale along the edges of the shell holes, tripping us.

A shell exploded near us, and we fell, faces into potato tops.

"Brothers," we heard a soft groaning voice.

Samokhin lifted his earth-smeared face, and I followed suit. Right next to us, only five steps away, a soldier lay on his back. His boxcalf boots told me that he was a sergeant. His shoulder boards confirmed that he was a master sergeant.

"Brothers . . ." he repeated.

"What do you want?" Samokhin got up on his knees and pulled his cap back on his head. "Are you wounded?"

"Shoot me, brothers," he rasped.

We came over meekly.

The sergeant's stomach was open, and the intestines spilled out in blue coils onto his bloodstained shirt and onto the black, crumbly soil. Flies were crawling on the intestines.

His eyes were rolling up. His breath came out in noisy gasps from the corners of his cracked mouth.

Samokhin chewed his lip, turned, and walked away. But I was rooted to the spot. The dying man's eyes stopped on me.

"Sonny . . . do a good deed. . . . Don't abandon me alive."

I felt a chill.

"I'm a goner," he said hoarsely. "And I can't be carried. . . . Have mercy. . . . Don't let me suffer. . . . Shoot me. . . ."

I shook my head and started backing away.

"What are you running off for, you viper?" I heard. "Too lazy . . . to help a man?"

And then I heard Samokhin. He came over to the dying man.

9

"Wait, don't make noise."

He slowly began taking his carbine strap from his shoulder.

"Now you're a man," the sergeant gasped. "Go on, brother. Don't drag it out."

Samokhin held the carbine in his right hand, and with his left removed his cap and covered the dying man's face. Then he placed the carbine's barrel against the cap.

"Thanks, pal," came the muffled words from under the cap.

The shot rang out. The earth trembled under my feet. I ran. Then I stopped and waited for Samokhin. He was wending his way slowly through the potato field, the carbine's strap dragging. Shells whistled over our heads several times. Unlike me, Samokhin did not fall to the ground. He kept on moving as if he were deaf. Then a shell exploded near us, and I fell into the hole. Samokhin slid down after me. The carbine followed down the crumbling side.

Samokhin remained on his knees and, without looking at me, stared at the empty sky.

"Lord," he whispered. "You alone are the judge."

I felt nauseated, and a stream of vomit spurted from my mouth onto the soft black earth, which bulged with white potatoes.

Part I

1

The Soviet Union was totally unprepared for World War II and at first suffered great defeats. The army fled from battlefields leaving behind tanks that had no ammunition and planes that had no fuel. The only person in that enormous country fully prepared for war was me, even though I was only nine years old. I was prepared by my mother, who knew nothing about politics, who listened to music and not news on the radio, and who used unread newspapers to light the stove.

My mother was a woman of solid build, stern morals, and great vanity. She was not only my mother, but also an athlete, a champion sprinter in the military region where my father was stationed. He was a commander of a cavalry-artillery division of the workers' and peasants' Red Army. The region was the westernmost in the USSR, near the Polish border, and as long as I can remember, the troops there were almost always on maneuvers, getting ready for war, which was expected any day.

Jewish mothers usually spoil their children. They overfeed them and don't let anyone bully them, defending them like angry tigresses, even when they are in the wrong.

But we were not like other people. Mama could not bear weak, whiny children who could not stand up for themselves, especially if they were boys. Mama despised me. She simply could not accept me. Only a conqueror could hope to attain her love. And I always returned from fights with local street kids with a swollen lip, a black eye, and scratches on my face. And, of course, in tears.

Any other Jewish mother, seeing her child in that state, would wail all over the street, wring her hands in grief, and rush outside to teach those bullies a lesson they'd never forget for hurting her darling.

But when I came home beaten up, I tried to keep out of Mama's way. Silently, knitting her brows and crossing her strong, trained arms over her chest, she would burn me with a cold, ruthless gaze, while I stumbled toward her on legs that refused to obey me, wiping blood and tears and suppressing the sobs that were bursting to escape my scrawny chest.

And so she would wait, arms crossed, until I made my way over to her, and when my forehead was practically pushing against her stomach, she would open her compressed lips.

"You're a girl, not a boy! A pathetic twerp! If you

can't stand up for yourself, don't stick your nose out on the street."

This was where I would lose control and burst out in bitter racking sobs. This didn't soften Mama's heart one bit. She grabbed my ear with her iron fingers, and the pain it caused eclipsed everything that had hurt before: my aching ribs and swollen lip. I felt my ear burst into flames beneath her fingers.

"Go back outside," she ordered, without raising her voice. "And don't come back until you teach those bullies a lesson. Understand? They have to be afraid of you and run when they see you. Go!"

She let go of my ear and gave me a resounding whack on the back of the head. I flew out, my feet barely keeping up.

Our neighbors, the wives of junior commanders from the division, could not hold back the tears as they watched from their windows, and abused my mother behind her back: "And you call that a mother! She should be the division commander instead of her husband."

I would fly out into the street, where they were already waiting for me, and fling myself into a fight three against one, and sometimes five against one. Blows showered upon me. I would fall, get back up, and strike out to the left and right, half blinded by blood, sweat, and tears—until they knocked me down again.

There was no place to retreat. I was more afraid of my mother than of the punches from the boys. My body grew hard and strong in the fights, and my punches grew more precise and powerful every time.

I stopped fighting blindly and began selecting a target to knock my opponent off his feet.

The day came when I beat up three boys, and they ran to hide in their houses, behind the backs of their mothers, who were cursing and swearing at me. Staggering with exhaustion, my shirt torn at the shoulder, my nose squashed and aching, I came down the empty street and saw my mother coming to meet me. She didn't praise me, but simply wiped my nose with her hankie and took me by the arm. My heart stopped with joy. I had never received a higher honor in my life.

"Wash up," Mama said briefly. "It's dinnertime."

Ever since then, I was the scourge of our street. No one dared mess with me, and I never touched anyone without a good reason.

Then Father's division was moved to a new city, and the new street where we were housed quickly recognized my strength. I was agile and flexible. I climbed tall trees like a monkey, holding on to the rough bark with my hands and feet. And I tore my clothes so fast that my mother could never keep enough in stock. She would smack me so hard that it made me fly several feet to the side. But I didn't fall, I managed to stay on my feet. And that made my mother proud, and her anger abated.

I loved my mother with a desperate, hungry, unrequited love. Like a dog, I stared into her eyes, seeking a spark of warmth. But all I found in her beautiful gray eyes were icicles. She was lovely and attractive—I knew that even as a small child, and I secretly admired her. I wanted so much for her to embrace me, to hold me close to her, to put me on her lap, to caress my shaved head. I don't know, maybe my memory is faulty, but no matter how hard I try, I can't recall a single time when my mother kissed me as a child.

Every garrison where the division was stationed, even the crummiest one, had a stadium. A soccer field covered with trampled grass and dandelions, wooden bleachers that left a pile of splinters in your behind, and a running track of fine gravel, circling the field and separating it from the bleachers.

That gravel track was the place where my love for my mother and my pride in her reached unthinkable heights.

Because here my mother was queen.

A shelf in our apartment held trophies of bronze running women on wooden stands with my mother's name engraved on them—prizes she won over the years before and after I was born. With our frequent moves, the trophies were packed first, and then the dishes were packed into a crate with wood shavings. Not only the bronze running women were packed, but also the muscular athletes with the same name engraved on their metal plaques. Those were Father's prizes. He was an even more famous athlete than Mama.

I never once saw my father perform. He trained at the base gyms, and he traveled to big cities for meets: to Minsk, Kiev, Leningrad, and Moscow. He defended the honor of the Red Army team. And his name appeared in newspapers, and Mama bought up the papers at the news kiosks and saved them in a separate suitcase.

At school both the boys and girls gave me openly

envious looks, as if the papers had written about me personally, and the teachers, even the toughest ones, gave me easy questions when they called on me and often gave me "excellent" when I didn't know my lesson at all.

In the summer the division left the base for temporary camps, deep in the woods. There were green lakes and pure streams that ran down the mossy rocks and golden sand to the large Berezina River, which lazily carried rafts as large as floating islands and steamboats with tall smokestacks through the forests and swamps.

Military training coincided with my school vacations, and wild with happiness, I left the town with the endless line of cannons pulled by horses. The division was sent off to bivouac by the whole town. From the sidewalks pretty girls waved lace hankies at the artillery gunners, pearly-toothed guys who sat astride the gun barrels. Older people and kids threw flowers at the artillery gunners and the cavalrymen, usually purple and white lilacs, which were in bloom at that time of year.

At the head of the column on a raven steed, saluting smartly, rode my father, his chest crisscrossed with gunbelts. And in front of Father, on a soft pillow attached to the horn of the saddle, melting and dissolving with joy, was I, waving a bouquet of lilacs over my shaved head, in a starched white shirt with a red Pioneer tie around my neck.

That was the tradition: A child led the parade riding in the commander's saddle and holding a bouquet.

The clatter of hoofs and the rattle of the metal wheels broke off on the outskirts of town: The cobblestoned street ended and we rode out onto the sand of the road that led to the damp woods.

Father rode onto the side of the road, letting the column pass, inspecting closely every gun, every cart. The soldiers, as they came level with him, dropped their chatter and straightened up, and only the most daring winked at me so that Father wouldn't notice.

Father took me off his horse, lifting me high in the air, handed me to some of his men. He guessed my secret desire to ride on the gun carriage, and I was thrilled when the soldiers moved over to seat me on the sun-warmed metal of the carriage.

The men adored my father, even though he was strict and tough. Hanging around the camp all summer, I overheard what the men talked about among themselves. Like me, the soldiers were proud of him. He was more than their commander. Commanders are feared and rarely loved. But none of the neighboring units had a commander like him. He was the best athlete in his division and in the whole military region. None of our soldiers ever entertained the thought of challenging him.

One evening, back from target practice, the men herded the horses to bathe in the river. They took me along.

The sun was setting beyond the distant forest, lighting copper tints on the pines of our bank. Ahead was a meadow, overgrown with sedge, and a fog was rolling in, its light, transparent clumps floating over the water. The heads of the horses sometimes seemed to dissolve in milk.

We swam next to the horses, bumping into their ribs underwater, and when we were tired, we climbed up on their wet backs, rested, and then dove into the foggy blanket, the splashes rising above the fog. Laughter and shouts mingled with neighs and splashes.

Then the voices began to quiet down, leaving only the horses' neighs. I climbed up on a horse next to a naked soldier who was sitting there and staring at something in the distance ahead. The soldier picked me up under my slippery arms and stood me up in front of him on the horse.

A marvelous picture awaited me. Coming around the river's bend toward us was the top of a black horse head and beyond it a partially visible man with his tanned, muscular legs in the air. His head, arms, and torso were hidden by fog. Only his shorts and legs were clear. The man was doing a headstand on the back of a swimming horse, and that's how they made their way through the fog to us. The soldiers and I immediately recognized the horse and upside-down rider. We were dumb with delight.

When Father and Demon were abreast of us, he jumped and stood on his horse's back, and his naked audience applauded with wet hands and hoots of pleasure. There was such love and devotion on our faces that if Father had asked the soldiers to die for him, I'm sure they would have done it on the spot.

He merely nodded sternly, his upper body showing over the fog, and said curtly:

"March to shore! It's almost lights-out."

No wonder my mother maintained that we were not like other people.

Even the building where we lived shortly before the war was not quite ordinary. It had been built so that if military action began, it could easily be turned into a hospital. That's why it didn't have a single normal apartment. They all lacked kitchens and toilets.

The families of commanders in the Red Army lived there. Our apartment was the best and contained two rooms. In case of war, it would be the operating room—all that was required was removing the partition between the rooms. All the other apartments on the floor consisted of a single square room—future wards for the wounded. They opened on a broad corridor. In the corridor in front of every door stood a stool, and on every stool a bottled-gas stove. Pots and pans were boiling and frying away under the eagle eyes of the housewives on guard duty—the officers' wives or mothers.

There was one toilet for the whole floor, at the very end of the corridor, and even I could understand that. The wounded wouldn't need toilets—they lie around in casts and use bedpans.

When the war in fact did begin, they didn't have time to turn our building into a hospital as planned. Our building and the whole city surrendered to the Germans in the very first days. Perhaps the Germans turned it into a hospital for their wounded—I don't know.

At the end of the corridor, next to the toilet, was the room of the only bachelor on our floor—Senior Lieutenant Manko, called the Horse Doctor. He was a veterinarian and in a cavalry division. That was a more important profession for the division than a people doctor. It's no secret that people can't carry heavy weapons very far, while horses will take them wherever you want. Manko loved horses more than people. I even knew why, because of all the people in our building, he confided in me alone.

"A horse, as opposed to a man," he told me once, moving his tobacco-stained finger under my nose, "won't betray you, but will repay kindness in double."

People on our floor didn't like Manko and were afraid of him.

He was a terrible drunkard and thus set a bad example for the family men. That's what the wives and mothers thought, and they unanimously turned their backs to Manko and their faces to their stoves when he walked down the corridor, exuding a stink of alcohol that killed all the smells coming from the pots and pans.

The fact that I befriended Manko and visited him when my mother wasn't looking earned me the housewives' enmity.

"Such parents," they wailed behind me, "and to have such a . . . God forgive me."

At that time my relations were not the best with my parents. They sat at the table talking in low voices. When I came closer, they'd stop and give me suspicious looks. Even at night they would whisper and check several times to see if I was asleep.

People were arrested at night, when I was asleep, and so I had never seen it happen, until they came for my father. But that was later. And Father, sensing that it would happen, called Mama every evening before coming home to find out if there was an ambush waiting in the apartment.

In my school, desks were emptying too. When a student didn't show up, everything was clear: His father was arrested, the family on its way to Siberia.

It wasn't like that just in our town, but all over the country, from the Baltic Sea to the Pacific Ocean. Later they called this period the Great Terror. Stalin was ruthlessly destroying his rivals and anyone else who got in the way, so that the rest would be afraid. He had millions of people shot or sent to Siberia. It all seemed like a scary, exciting game that the grown-ups were playing: the executioners and the victims. And we children wanted to be part of the game.

In our family the game began with a group photo. It showed three rows of Father's military comrades with whom he had studied in Moscow. Father sat among them on the floor. All of them, as befits senior officers, had stern, stony faces.

Once I noticed that one of the heads in the picture was covered by a round piece of white paper. I asked Father why. He told me embarrassedly that the man, a commander of a brigade in the Far East, turned out to be a Japanese spy and had been exposed by state security. He covered up the second spy—this time a Polish one—with me, and I helped cut out a circle. I liked this game. The people in the picture were losing their heads. The shoulders were there, the heads were there, even their feet were visible—like that Polish spy, who sat shoulder to shoulder in the front row with Father. But now instead of heads they had white balloons. Mother and Father did not share my delight. They didn't even smile.

Almost every day we had to cover up the face of an enemy, and the number of white circles kept growing, threatening to fill the whole picture. My father was surrounded by enemies. And suddenly a needle pierced my mind—what if tomorrow in some other house a boy covered up my dear father's face?

Asking my parents about all this was a waste of time; they just changed the subject. That left only one person I could talk to—Horse Doctor Manko.

"What's there not to understand?" Manko sneered, wiping his mouth after draining a shot glass of vodka. "Stalin is chopping down Russia. At the root. Wait—and he'll reach your father. A good man isn't going to stay free for long in our times."

The words chilled me to the bone. I couldn't believe it, even though I knew that Manko wasn't kidding around.

Veterinarian Manko was usually drunk. And as my mother says, what a drunk has in his mind goes out his lips. Manko was a very lonely man. He worked with the horses from morning till night. He talked to them, never had a kind word for people. He'd come home, lock himself in his room, drink the alcohol he brought back from the veterinary pharmacy; and if he didn't start playing the flute, he'd get rowdy and start a fight in the corridor. He wasn't afraid of anyone except Mama.

"Manko!" she would say to him calmly, while the other women from our floor hid behind her. "Back to your room!"

"Yessir, comrade commander. Allow me to kiss your hand, ma'am." He always obeyed her.

"Clown," my mother would say and turn away from him, going back to our apartment. Manko would crawl back to his lair under the hateful gaze of the women.

My mother often told Father that Manko should be sent to hell, that he was a disgrace to the division. Father agreed with her, but he left the veterinarian alone. He forgave him all his outbursts, because Manko had golden hands and the kindest heart for horses. There wasn't a better specialist in the whole military region, and my father would rather have lost an arm than Horse Doctor Manko.

When theater companies arrived in our town on tour, they used local talent to make up their orchestras, and our Manko was always the flutist.

Once I saw him rehearsing his part, and it was all I could do to keep from laughing. He was sitting in front of a folding music stand with the sheet music, holding the flute to his lips, and without making a single sound, beating out the measures with his foot. He beat a long time and then whistled a bit. Then he tapped some more. Then another soft whistle.

"You see," he said, "I have to wait sixteen measures before I come in."

"To whistle once?" I was amazed.

"I play one note. The oboe plays one. The clarinet

25

adds one. And the violin knows when to come in. Together, it makes the overture. A pleasure for the ears."

Lately Manko had stopped rehearsing. They weren't making up orchestras anymore. Half the musicians had been arrested. Commanders were vanishing with greater frequency from our building, followed by their families. Fear gripped all the floors. The housewives stopped chatting around their portable stoves—God forbid you might let slip the wrong thing and get your man into trouble. People stopped visiting each other. They locked themselves up in their rooms and sat like mice, listening to the radio. All it played was information on trials of "enemies of the people," and the sentences were all the same—the most severe punishment, execution by shooting. You listened to the radio and it seemed that the black box was shooting machine-gun volleys and people were dropping like flies. Not just ordinary people, but celebrities known throughout the land.

There were more and more empty seats in our school, and the class looked like a mouth that had lost a lot of teeth. But the children whose families had not yet been declared "enemies of the people" came to class as if nothing were wrong, and even misbehaved in class and went crazy at recess, like in the good old days.

We were caught up in spy mania. We were dying to show our patriotism and demonstrate our love and loyalty to our Soviet Homeland and Comrade Stalin himself, the way Pavlik Morozov had. He was a boy just like us, but a hero, renowned throughout the land. He had been killed by the enemy for denouncing his own father to the authorities. His father was arrested, and the boy was hacked to death by his own grandfather.

We Soviet children wept for Pavlik Morozov and at the same time were eaten with jealousy for his fame. Everyone wanted to be him. We were ready to die without regret in such a heroic death. But that required something not every boy was capable of—turning over his own father to torture and death.

At school they lined us up under an enormous portrait of Pavlik Morozov, and we gave our solemn Pioneer vow to be just as patriotic as the hero boy from the distant Urals. Pavlik's picture appeared in all the newspapers and magazines and was even sold as a postcard in the school kiosk. I bought one with my lunch money and brought it home. I showed it to my parents at dinner and they exchanged a look. They *knew* about Pavlik.

"All that is very good," Mother said, "but make sure your interest in this . . . boy doesn't affect your schoolwork. You're very impressionable, you know."

"If it's necessary," I repeated the words from our vow given before his portrait, "I will also give up my life like Pavlik Morozov."

Mama and Father looked at each other again and Father asked softly, "Necessary for whom?"

"The Homeland," I said curtly.

Mama and Father exchanged a third look and then looked away. They didn't look at me at all for the rest of the meal. And I didn't dare look into their eyes. We ate in silence, like strangers. I realized that they did not trust me anymore and were even afraid of me. But instead of being pleased by my discovery—for now our roles had changed, and they were afraid of me—I felt shame, and tears welled in my eyes. I wanted to rush to them and hug them and tell them that they needn't doubt me, I wouldn't turn them in . . . because my parents couldn't be enemies of the people. Others could, but not my parents.

I nailed the picture of Pavlik Morozov to the wall over my bed. My parents noticed it, but said nothing. They just exchanged another look. That evening was the first time they forgot to wish me a good night. I fell asleep anxiously and had bad dreams.

When I returned from school, the picture was gone from the wall above my bed. There was nothing but the hole.

"Where is it?" I asked, giving my mother an uncompromising look, which I imagined was appropriate to a contemporary of Pavlik Morozov's.

I saw that my mother was itching to slap my face, but she controlled herself, which was something new, and instead of answering my question, said with iron in her voice:

"I categorically forbid hammering nails into the wall. Bedbugs live in the holes."

And turning her back to me, she made it clear that the conversation was ended.

The hero's picture disappeared without a trace, and I didn't dare buy another.

I reported all this to my friend, Horse Doctor Manko, dropping in on him in the evening, and he listened to my complaints about my parents without interrupting, merely wheezing alcohol breath at me and staring at the floor under his bare feet. His dusty boots stood nearby, the tops drooping wearily.

"Are you finished?" he asked when I stopped, and then raised his swollen eyes. "You're a fool, my friend. You're not a small child. You're going to be chasing young ladies soon. But you don't have a penny's worth of brains."

I was stunned, but I didn't give up. I hotly defended myself, quoting the words of the teacher and the Pioneer leader.

"Don't listen to anyone. Understand?" Manko said grimly. "Otherwise you'll grow up to be a vile, low-down person, and I'll be ashamed to have known you. You can't trade your father for an idea, no matter how wonderful it might be. Beat that into your little head! There is nothing higher than a father! His blood is in you. Your roots are in him. You are one, indivisible. If you cut down the root, you'll wilt yourself. That Pavlik Morozov of yours . . . is scum! Get him out of your head! Don't soil your thoughts with his lousy name."

I sat glued to my seat. No one had ever said anything like that to me. No one would dare pronounce such words around a witness. Only Manko, a totally fearless man, could attack my idol and trample him ruthlessly.

"It's not true, all that," he said after a pause. "A child's soul isn't capable of such vileness. They just made up the story . . . those big grown-up bastards, to set you small fry against your fathers."

"Manko," I said, barely breathing. "For words like that . . . do you know what could happen to you?"

29

"Go tell on me. You'll get your picture in the paper. Go on, get out of here!"

I left, but I didn't go home. I went into the toilet, which was next to Manko's room, and gave in to my tears. I was completely confused. I didn't know whom to believe, what was good, what was bad, who was friend, who was foe.

I didn't stop visiting Manko. He didn't bear a grudge, and the next time I knocked on his door, he let me in as if nothing had happened, and we were still friends.

That drunkard, rejected by everyone, opened my eyes to life, and for that I was grateful to him forever. For I began to recognize and understand some of the flood of lies the country was drowning in.

Manko was a prophet—the time soon came for my family to suffer the sorrow that was blanketing the country. Nothing saved my father—not his immaculate service record, not his success as an athlete.

Three men came in secret-police uniforms: boots, blue jodhpurs, and gray military raincoats.

Their faces were as gray as their coats. They burst into our apartment toward morning. They brought along a witness, our neighbor, half-dressed Major Pipko, who blinked sleepily and stared at his former superior, my father, with guilt.

When I was awakened by strange voices in the apartment and padded barefoot into the dining room, I saw those three in boots and my father in his underwear. Mama wore a robe and pressed close to Father's shoulder. They were frozen, motionless, and they had faces like stone statues.

One of the three opened a military map case, looked at the paper, and asked the question:

"Your last name?"

Father and Mother did not respond. They remained standing like statues.

"I repeat. What is your last name?"

And then Mama moved. She brought her palm to her temple and looked helplessly at Father.

"What's our last name?" she asked him. "I can't remember."

Father was looking at her. His lips moved. But I couldn't hear any sound.

"How silly." I giggled from behind the door that was ajar. "Can't remember our name. All right, I'll help."

And I told the visitors our name, loudly, as if reciting in class. They didn't ask any other questions, but began a thorough search, turning the apartment upside down. They even looked inside the hollow trophies.

Then they ordered Father to get dressed and pack a change of underwear, and they took him away.

The door slammed behind him, boots clattered on the stairs, moving ever lower, from floor to floor. The front door thudded, and a car hummed as it pulled away from our building.

When they took Father away, it was still dark outside. Mother didn't go back to bed. She tucked me in, but I couldn't fall asleep either. I listened tensely, expecting another knock on the door. We knew that they would come for us to take us to Siberia—the family of an "enemy of the people."

I was surprised that Mama just sat indifferently among our scattered things, touching nothing after the search. At least she could have packed for our trip. If they came for us, there wouldn't be time to pack. But Mother sat like a stone in her robe and stared out the dark window, without moving or blinking.

The knock came when it was growing light outside, a stealthy, quiet knock. I jumped in my bed. Mother didn't stir. There was another knock.

"It's not locked," she said without turning.

Manko came in, in a quilted jacket, boots, and hat. He looked as if he were about to set out on a long journey. He shut the door soundlessly behind him.

"Manko!" Mama exclaimed. "Aren't you afraid to visit us? We're enemies of the people, you know."

And she wept silently, so the neighbors wouldn't hear. I couldn't remember Mama ever crying. That scared me.

Manko embraced her and tenderly patted her back, repeating, "Don't cry, don't cry. . . ."

"What else can I do?"

"Get ready . . . for the trip. . . . You have a sister on the Volga. . . . Leave immediately."

"They won't let us out."

"That's not your concern. Hurry! Time is against us."

He had already been down to the stables and had driven his trap to the building.

We tiptoed down the stairs. Manko carried my sleeping sister. In the driveway Demon—my father's personal horse—pawed the ground impatiently. Mama barely kept herself from wailing out loud when she saw Demon. Why had Manko hitched up Demon? He believed that horses were more sensitive than people; apparently he wanted to give Demon a chance to say good-bye.

As we left the military town, the guard raised the striped tollgate and saluted Manko.

"They're . . . with me," Manko announced, to cut off any curiosity from the guards.

Mama realized at the train station that we didn't have any money for the tickets. The last fifty rubles we had in the house were taken during the search.

"That's not your concern," Manko said, and went to buy the tickets.

The train arrived, and I saw for the first time how a human says good-bye to a horse. My mother put her arms around Demon's swanlike neck and, holding back her sobs, kissed the smooth mane of Father's horse. And you can believe me or not, but Demon shed a tear. A tear the size of a pea rolled down from his large eye.

Manko gave us each an alcohol hug and seated us in the car.

We never saw him again. His turn came too. I learned that from someone else. He was also taken away at night, but not quietly. He was the only one in our building to resist arrest, and he was beaten as they dragged him down the corridor and then down the stairs. There was never another word about him. I guess he was killed during the interrogation. People like Manko don't give up without a fight.

It was 1937. The year of Stalin's terrible purges. Hundreds of thousands of innocent people all over Russia were disappearing at night from their apartments, never to return. The worst losses were borne by the Red Army, which was left without officers on the eve of the war.

And I was left without a father.

My generation considers our childhood to have ended in 1941 when the war began. My childhood ended when I was only nine years old.

2

The village where my aunt's husband worked as an agronomist was located far from the railroad station. We knew from their letters that in the spring and fall, when the rivers flooded, it was cut off from the world. The only form of communication was the telephone, which was usually out of service. Now all those inconveniences were advantages. We would be lost, like needles in a haystack, and wait for better times. The nightmare had to end sometime, or Russia would be left without any people. Then we would reappear and start looking for Father to see if he had managed to survive the camps.

It was winter. As our train traveled east, it got colder, and the track was surrounded by tall snowbanks blown by the wind. There were no forests around the Volga, only miles and miles of endless steppes, covered with snow like a clean white sheet.

We rattled across the bridge over the Volga, and far below us there was solid ice. Then we got off at some tiny station, roof deep in snow, and a little old man drove us in a sled to Auntie's village, first piling up handfuls of straw over the three of us to keep us from freezing.

We spent the night and half the next day in the creaking sled, and we did not come across a living soul. That's how far away we were, and the farther the hoar-covered horse pulled us, the brighter my mother's face grew. For we wanted to get away, to bury ourselves as deep as possible in this endless snow.

Auntie greeted us with the news that she had also become a "grass widow," the wife of an "enemy of the people." Her husband the agronomist had been arrested and taken away.

There was nowhere to go from here. We couldn't take my mother's sister anywhere anyway—her swollen stomach was bursting through her dress. She was going to have a baby any day.

The two sisters wept in each other's arms and decided to await their fate together in Auntie's cold hut made of adobe brick—crumbly lumps of clay mixed with straw. In the steppe there are no logs, nor any coal. Here there are straw houses that are heated with burning straw. The agronomist had been planning to bring in a wagonload, but he was arrested before he had the chance, and so the house was left without fuel. Auntie did not poke her nose outside, and people made a point of avoiding the "enemy" agronomist's house.

My mother decided to go see the village authorities. No matter how afraid people might be, they wouldn't let a pregnant woman freeze in an unheated house. The authorities, avoiding her eyes, agreed with my mother and allowed her to borrow a pair of horses from the stable for half a day to bring in straw from the steppe haystacks.

That was easy to say, borrow the horses. Neither my aunt nor my mother had ever dealt with horses and did not know how to treat them. I knew how to ride horseback—I learned when my father took me to camp in the summer with his cavalry-artillery division.

But there was no way out. The two horses were exhausted and worn out, with sagging backs and curly shaggy-haired bellies. The stable groom hitched up the horses to a sled, under a yoke, handed me the reins and said, "Git!"

"Get in, Mama," I invited.

My mother gave me a suspicious look from under her frozen eyelashes, checked how I held the reins, and sat down next to me.

I jiggled the reins, whistled, and shouted, and the horses set off at different times. The sled, its runners frozen to the snow, lurched forward. The runners squeaked along the ruts in the snowy roads. And we were off.

The day was cold and sunny. The ruts in the road glistened, and our sled glided easily past the telegraph posts. The low houses of the village with their dark thatched roofs were left behind, while ahead as far as the eye could see lay the winter steppe, a white sea with white frozen waves of drifts. The huge haystacks rose in that vast expanse like ships in the sea.

I was told to take hay from the sixth haystack on the right side of the road, and I tried counting them, squinting in the unbearable snow reflections of the sun. Sleigh tracks turned off the road to the sixth stack—others had taken hay there before us—and I headed for the tracks. The horses shifted from a canter to a walk, trying to step into the deep holes made by the other horses' hoofs. They had worked up a sweat, and steam rose from their shaggy backs. Now, as they cooled off, they were quickly covered in lacy hoarfrost.

I felt like a man, the head of the family, and so I became taciturn and even grim. Mother sat next to me, also silent. She smiled quietly, staring straight ahead. Ever since we had been left alone without Father, I had often seen that meaningless smile frozen on her face. Instinctively I feared it. I was afraid she was losing her mind and would burst out laughing wildly, unable to stop, and they would take her away to the hospital. And my sister and I would be left all alone. Auntie didn't count. She was barely breathing out of fear, and she was pregnant and didn't have time for us.

By the time we reached the haystack, Mama and I were quite chilled, and we moved fast and hard loading the hay onto the cart. I climbed up on the stack and used a pitchfork to toss down bunches of flattened hay that smelled like bread. The straw was gray on top but golden on the inside, and when I lifted it over my head, a tickling golden dust fell on me. I got overheated, and sweat poured into my eyes. But I was happy that I was strong and could lift such man-sized forkfuls of hay and throw them down to Mama, sometimes covering her from head to toe. I laughed and she frowned without anger and brandished her fist at me.

When the pile of hay in the sled seemed big enough, I jumped down onto it from the haystack. Mama tossed up a thick rope to me, which was attached to the back of the sled. I tied it to the front. Then we both climbed up. Like an adult, I helped my mother up.

The first thing I discovered as I picked up the reins was that the sleigh tracks leading back to the road were gone. Streams of dry snow swirled around the horses' feet, filling in the tracks. The wind pinched my cheeks. Way on the horizon I could barely make out tiny matchsticks that were the telegraph poles. That's where the road was, and that's where I headed the horses.

The sleigh lurched, the runners came away from the ice, and we were off. The horses stepped into the loose snow, sometimes sinking to their bellies, but they kept hauling us. Both the animals and we were afraid of the quickly approaching night and the ever-increasing wind. It was the start of a blizzard.

Soon the matchstick telegraph poles were gone, as if the wind mixed with snow had licked them away. Mother was the first to sense danger and kept looking around anxiously. I kept urging on the horses with shouts. The poles had been the last landmarks, and now I had to depend on the horses. They could sense where the house was and head for it themselves.

The sleigh shook dangerously as we went in and out

of the deep drifts. At times it felt as if we were about
to keel over. Mama hugged me close. I poked my nose
against her cold cheek and felt her lips moving.

"Are you praying?" My eyelashes were frozen.
Mother's cheek slid along my nose: She smiled.

"No, son. Even if I wanted to pray, I don't know any
prayers. You and I are godless."

"Then what were you whispering?"

"I was talking to the horses, telling them to be good
and to bring us back, safe and sound."

"But they don't understand people talk."

"Who does?"

She lifted her face to the sky. I followed suit. Snow
whirled above us, howling and showering us with a
dust that stung like fine salt.

"Don't bother looking," I said. "There is no God."

"Silly boy," my mother sighed. "I'm looking for
stars. Travelers use stars to guide them."

"Father would know where to go," I said.

Mother sighed. "Where is he now? . . . Under what
stars?"

We weren't swaying anymore—the horses were
standing still. They were chest deep in a drift and their
lowered heads stuck out, barely visible in the snowfall.

I shouted at them and shook the reins.

The horses shuffled their feet and made an effort to
move the sleigh. They struggled uselessly, flounder-
ing in the snow.

"Get down, son. We'll help the horses," Mama said.

She slid down and ended up waist deep in snow. I
followed, jumping into her open arms.

We shouted at the horses, urging them on.

The horses struggled—snorting, kicking, they seemed to be trying to swim. But the sleigh was frozen.

"That's it," Mama said in a crestfallen voice when I came around the sleigh, almost up to my shoulders in the snow. "There's only one hope. To walk."

"What about the horses?"

"What about them?"

She stared unblinking into space, and I was frightened by her lifeless expression.

As long as I could remember, Mama had never despaired. She hadn't been this distracted and apathetic even during Father's arrest. I understood that we were in big trouble, and I didn't ask any more questions.

But her eyes cleared, squinted, and she compressed her lips. That's the way she looked at the stadium, on the track, when she crouched, ready to start. Mama called that state clenching your will into a fist.

Now, out in the steppes of the Volga region, in a whirlwind of snow that threatened to kill us both, Mother clenched her will into a fist, and I felt a little better.

"Follow me," she said, and moved away from the sleigh, pushing the snowdrifts apart with her arms.

She left a deep, solid path, a narrow crevice in the snow. I went through the crevice, the top of which came to my shoulders. It wasn't easy, because on my feet wobbled huge adult shoes, filled with straw for warmth. They had been left behind by the agronomist husband. Mama had ordered me to wear them, to keep my feet from freezing. They really were warm, but they were so heavy that it made walking difficult, and I tired quickly.

The blizzard wiped away all traces of the sleigh and horses. Now we could see nothing but the stream of stinging, swirling snow. If I fell back two or three steps, Mama's back in the gray army coat began to disappear, and shaggy, burning tongues of snow lashed out between us. I speeded up, and my forehead bumped into her back.

Mama never turned around, but she kept calling out: "Are you there?"

"Here," I replied, stumbling on the long skirts of my aunt's coat and barely moving my feet in her husband's enormous shoes.

"Are you there?"

"I've lost my shoe. The right one."

Mother came back, crouched, and ran her hands around in the snow.

"Where did you lose it? Do you remember?"

"No."

My right foot was just in its sock, and I pulled my leg up like a bird, afraid to set it down on the burning snow.

"You'll be the death of me," my mother said, bending over me. "Give me your foot. I'll put my mitten on it for now. Otherwise . . ."

She didn't finish. She put her wool mitten with one thumb sticking up on my foot and kept feeling around in the snow with her hand. I lay down on my back and raised my feet up, for a little rest.

The snow didn't sting anymore but caressed my face, and I shut my eyes. Somewhere above me the blizzard sang gently and sweetly, like a lullaby.

"Get up," I heard Mother's voice. "You can't lie down."

"Five more minutes," I begged through my sleepiness. "Just five more minutes."

That was what I usually said when mother woke me for school. And she shouted at me just the way she did every morning: "No minutes! Get up!"

She shook me roughly by the shoulders, and wrapped her scarf around my mittened foot, tying it tight around my knee.

"You won't freeze," she said, helping me onto my feet. "Give me your hand."

With her naked hand, cold and wet, she held mine and walked sideways, dragging me after her.

"There. Another step. Another. We'll be home soon. We'll light the stove. Boil some tea. Very very hot. And very very sweet."

We were walking against the wind. I was protected by my mother's back, which made it easier for me. She was bent double, stubbornly beating a path for us with her bare head.

"You're my man now," she said, breathing hard. "All grown up. The only one in the family. Our defender. What would we do without you?"

She was out of breath. Even her trained athlete's body was giving up. Her steps became smaller and less frequent. Then she stopped, her snow-white head dropping weakly to her chest. And I saw apathy in her eyes again. She was staring into space.

Fear stung me.

"Let's go, Mama," I said, pulling her hand. And I

went ahead. My shoulder dug into a drift, pushing aside the crumbling snow with my knees and elbows. Mama followed, quietly whispering: "A man . . . defender, the only one in the family."

I was gasping in the wind; the snow filled up my open mouth. But I used my last ounce of strength to push on.

Then, totally exhausted, we stood holding each other, and snow swirled above our heads, quickly mounting on our shoulders.

Mama held me close and as we rested we spoke.

"We shouldn't have left the horses," I said angrily. "We could have burrowed into the straw and waited out the storm. . . . It's warm in the straw."

"Twenty-twenty hindsight."

"Or even better . . . unhitched the horses and tried to ride to the village. The horses would have found the way."

"I can't ride."

"Well, then I would have gone and you would have stayed with the other horse, got into the straw, and waited warm and safe until I brought help."

"You don't wave your fists after a fight."

I was glad that Mother was answering. Her strength was coming back.

"Let's go."

"Where?" I asked. "Are you sure we're going the right way?"

"I'm not sure of anything," Mother replied. "Maybe we're just circling. But we have to keep moving . . . anywhere. We can go left if you like, or right."

While we had been standing, the snow covered us,

and even three feet away visibility was nothing—just murky white porridge: from above, on all sides, and in back of us.

We went on, holding hands. I limped. My foot bound in Mother's scarf got stuck in the snow, and it was hard to pull it out. My strength was ebbing. I couldn't hold my head up. I was falling asleep on my feet. Then I tripped and fell. The snow stuck to my eyes, my nose, my mouth. I barely had the strength to roll over onto my back. And immediately I felt bliss. I shut my eyes in sweet languor. In my sleep, far, far away, I could hear Mother. My body was swaying from side to side.

"Go on, Mama, go without me," I moaned, pulling away from her. "I'll sleep. . . . I feel so warm. . . ."

"You're dying," she said. "This is the end."

She did not shout. She spoke those words in a very ordinary way. And maybe that was why I opened my eyes.

Mama stood over me, reaching toward the sky. From below I could see only her elbows, her chin, and the tip of her nose. And I heard her voice. It sounded like a moan.

"Lord!" My mother was calling to the murky sky. "If You do exist in the sky . . . You won't abandon an orphan. . . ."

I was the orphan, and she was talking to God. My mother was talking to God.

I knew that she didn't believe in any God and had taught me not to. She had been a member of the Komsomol before I was born, the wife of a Communist who was a commander in the Red Army. And now she was raising her hands to heaven, giving up, capitulating, in a last attempt to be saved.

"You won't abandon an orphan."

I was afraid. I realized that Mama and I were on the brink of death if words like that fell from her lips. So I jumped up, by myself.

"Let's go, Mama."

The rest was like a dream. We swam instead of walking, drowning in drifts and swimming out of them. Dragging each other and panting like exhausted horses. I thought that steam was coming from our blazing faces.

Then Mama suddenly was hanging on something, seemingly spread out in the air. I grabbed her coat from behind and pulled. Mama was hanging in the air and crying, wailing the way they do at funerals:

"We're saved! We're alive! We're going to live!"

I went around my mother, pushing my chest and knees through the heavy snow, and saw that she was lying on a black iron cross, hanging like one crucified. It was a graveside cross. And looking around, I saw other crosses, a fence of crosses.

We were at the cemetery. We had come upon the dead.

"We're alive!" Mama wept, embracing the cross. "Where the dead are, the living can't be far. We've reached the village."

My chin began to tremble, and I was starting to cry too. My tears mixed with the snow, and my eyes searched the sky. No stars were visible, but perhaps there lived someone who had heard my mother's repentant prayer.

3

War is etched in a single image in the memory of everyone who has experienced it, often not the most horrible of everything that was seen. My childhood mind soaked up and retained many things. But even now when I look back, recalling my wartime childhood, I always see one thing.

That was the bone. With a jagged break. A human bone, a leg bone. The yellowish bone stuck up out of a black army boot, laced up and standing normally, as if the person whose foot it was had been running and lost the boot along with the foot.

There was no blood, and there was nothing else remaining of that person. Only the black boot and the naked yellow bone staring at the sky. It stood on an empty plank platform of a train station that had just been bombed. There wasn't a single intact pane in the tall windows. Sharp shards protruded from the corners of the frames. Ground glass lay on the window-sills. They had managed to haul the burning trains to sidings, where they let them burn. The bodies had been picked up and taken away. The survivors were still hiding in bomb shelters and cellars, waiting to see if the bombers would return.

I was first to clamber out onto the deserted platform. That's when I saw the boot with the worn heel and the jagged yellow bone.

That is how my memory visualizes war. Now my childhood and the war are far behind. But back then I was twelve, I was left alone for the first time, without my parents, without my teachers. Without supervision. All alone in the world.

On the empty tracks in front of the station a black oil tanker smoldered, giving off a suffocating smoke. Between the tank and station on the platform's concrete stood a white, prewar kiosk, with a long line of people leading to it like a snake. Refugees: dusty women with grimy children in their arms, old men and old women, so ancient they must have crawled out of the grave. Militiamen in blue uniforms with green gas masks dangling from their hips were regulating the unruly line, all the while glancing up at the sky.

"What? Another raid?" a toothless old woman muttered.

"Yes, granny," I said, "an air raid."

The old woman didn't hear a damn thing. I was behind her in the line to the kiosk. Kiosks like this were working overtime at all the stations I passed. They were food points for refugees, evacuees.

You could stuff yourself with the tastiest things, cranberry jelly, rice gruel. Of course, for the best food you had to be either an infant or a very, very old person—a God's dandelion, ready to blow off at any moment. For the rest of us there were sausages, cheese sandwiches, and hot borsch with sour cream if you had your own bowl.

But I didn't like what I was given. I preferred the cranberry jelly or the sweet rice gruel, handed out in semitransparent bumpy bottles, marked off from top to bottom with lines and numbers to make it easy to see how much you consumed in one gulp and how much was left.

As neither infant nor old man I was supposed to get sausages and sandwiches. But I had already learned to fool grown-ups. I was a perfect liar.

Somewhere in the distance the steam engines howled, sounding like barking dogs. The air-raid signal. And in confirmation the station's siren cried, gathering strength. The militiamen on the platform shouted: "Air raid! Air raid!" The line shuddered and scattered, with many voices repeating: "Air raid! Air raid!" People ran, losing bags, kerchiefs, canes. Someone fell. They trampled him.

Everyone was running, even the militiamen. But I didn't run—I was an old hand. I saw the kerchief-covered head of the anxious distributor in the kiosk—she didn't dare leave her domain unattended. This wasn't her first bombing, either.

"Lady!" I shouted, so that she could hear me over the barking steam engines. "Gimme the parcel!"

"What parcel?" the woman said. "Run to the shelter! It's a raid! You'll come back for the parcel."

"I can't," I said, shaking my head right above the counter. "My family's hungry. My mother sent me."

"Lord! What kind of person is she? Sending a child! Couldn't she come herself?"

"No!" I shouted. "Babies!"

"Your mother's?"

"Who else? Twins."

The twins did it.

"Lord! At a time like this . . . twins . . ." she muttered, bending down behind the counter. She came up, hugging two pink and two white bottles to her ample bosom—cranberry jelly and rice drink. She placed the bottles on the counter under my nose, and next to it put sandwiches and sausages wrapped in cellophane.

"Feed your mother. . . . And there's some for you."

Those sandwiches were dead weight for me. I wouldn't eat them and I wouldn't carry them far from the kiosk—I was going to throw them away around the corner. I preferred to have more jelly and drink. Putting on a sad face and pumping as much honesty as I could into my gaze, I said:

"More jelly, please . . . and rice drink . . . for weak old people. . . . My grandpa and grandma are with us. . . . They have no teeth . . . they can't chew."

The distributor listened compassionately to my lies, sighed, and put four more bottles on the counter. I gathered up all eight bottles with both hands and pressed them to my chest.

"How will you carry the sandwiches?" she asked, her eyebrows flying up.

"What do I need them for?" I sneered brazenly, no more sadness in my eyes. "Eat them yourself."

I ran along the deserted platform to the barking of the distant steam engines and the endless siren's howl, which alternated between very high, almost squealing notes and a tired bass.

I ran to the brick water tower. No one about, and no sound of German planes in the sky. That meant they had passed to the side for a more important target. That meant another siren would go off soon signalling the end of the air raid. The crumpled refugees would come creeping out of everywhere—cellars, shelters, trenches hurriedly dug in the station square—and come running to the platform. To get a place in the line for the food distributor.

I sat on the hot ground at the foot of the brick water tower. Next to me were six bottles: three red and three white. Two empty ones lay on their sides. I ate without rushing, savoring every sip from two bottles at a time. A sip of the jelly, a sip of the rice drink. Saying: "This is for Grandpa. . . . And this is for Grandma. . . . And this is for one twin. . . . And this is for the other."

The empties hit the black dirt with a thunk. I felt my belly filling up and swelling. I felt drowsy with food and warmth. And my eyes could hardly stay open while I drained the last bottle.

My back was against the warm bricks. My head lolled

51

to one side. I heard the water rumbling. A black pipe extended from the tower, and a thin stream fell from its rusty, uneven end, splashing into a black puddle on the ground. I realized that this was an opportunity to wash at least my hands, which were covered with the gray-black dirt of several days. But I couldn't open my eyes. I was too lazy to move. I sank into a sweet sleep. I didn't even open my eyes when shells landed right by my ear and shrapnel fell from the sky like handfuls of peas.

I lay facedown on the hot, acrid-smelling asphalt. Feet trampled on the asphalt. Someone ran over me. I could hear the crunch of my ribs under the sole of his shoe.

Maybe those weren't my ribs cracking? I heard bullets making perforated lines in the asphalt. And a plane whining as it came out of its dive.

Was this delirium or reality?

Then I clearly saw the station square, its gray asphalt buckled, stinking of machine-gun rounds, and littered with piles of abandoned clothing. People were scattered everywhere, motionless, dead, facedown on the asphalt.

And I also saw the name of the city on the façade of the station, covered with black splotches of camouflage nets. Orel. I was in the city of Orel. Had I come that far? And so I lay on the station square, unable to understand whether I was dead or alive. I didn't feel pain anywhere. Actually, I didn't feel my body at all, as if it had been torn off. Only my head remained, throbbing and slow thinking.

Voices nearby. Above me.

"Dead on the left . . . in that pile. . . . And all the wounded in a row . . . easier to load."

"Where does this one go?"

"The kid?"

My heart skipped a beat—they were talking about me.

"Dead. Not moving."

"But there's no blood."

They picked me up. I wanted to scream that I was alive, but I couldn't.

"Hey, look, he's jerking."

"Breathing."

"He's sick. His forehead is burning."

"Where's the doctor? Maybe he's got typhus."

"We should look for his parents. His mother must be running around looking for him."

"Put him over here, to one side. Closer to the evacuees. Someone might recognize him."

Realizing that I was alive and, more importantly, that people around me knew I was alive and wouldn't bury me with the dead in the big pit that they call a fraternal grave, I fell into blessed oblivion.

I was back in prewar times, in my school with its windows flung open into the spring garden. The storm windows had just been removed, and the ceaseless babble of rooks, back from the south, filled the classroom. The sharp smells of the garden, as sharp as ethyl alcohol, awakened from a winter sleep, made us dizzy—we couldn't even hear our teacher, who was moving his lips silently. We called him the Walrus. The geography teacher, Ivan Alexandrovich.

The resemblance to a walrus came from Ivan Alex-

53

androvich's fat mustache, which drooped on both sides of his mouth below his chin, like a walrus's reddish tusks. Ivan Alexandrovich had a bald pate, yellow and covered with brown spots, and in the middle of his bald head, right on top, a hollow. We aimed at that hollow, shooting ink from the tips of our pens as soon as he turned his back to us. If we missed the hollow, the ink dribbled down his bald head.

We drove Ivan Alexandrovich crazy. He had been a teacher in the tsar's days, before the 1917 Revolution. When the Revolution got rid of the tsar, all the teachers from the tsar's time were shown the door as well.

But the Soviets allowed elderly Ivan Alexandrovich to stay on, to keep him from starving. He taught the most harmless subject, geography, and only to the lower grades.

There were times when Ivan Alexandrovich was just itching to whack us with a ruler, like in the good old days before the Revolution. He particularly wanted to hit me, his primary tormentor. Forgetting himself, he would sometimes grab the ruler from his desk and, beet red and spluttering under his mustache, he would raise his arm. Then, remembering, he would hide his hand with the ruler behind his back and bite his white lower lip with his long upper teeth.

He was not allowed to touch the children of workers and peasants—the hope and future of the country that was building communism. Especially me, the son of an officer in the worker-peasant Red Army.

All he could do was berate us. It wasn't customary in Soviet schools, but there was no law against scolding pupils. And Ivan Alexandrovich let off steam in curses, the likes of which you'll never hear anywhere else. What he called me! Brontosaurus, ichthyosaurus, pithecanthropus, Neanderthal. If I could remember all the names, I would pass a zoology exam. The stream of curses and names, mixed with saliva, would be interrupted by the bell announcing the end of class. Hearing the bell, he would stuff his fat, unshuttable briefcase under his arm and run from the room—most often carrying off a rolling drop of violet ink in the hollow on his skull.

Choking with laughter, we would hurry after him, pushing and shoving in the doorway, so as not to miss the moment when Ivan Alexandrovich greeted one of his colleagues in the hallway with old-fashioned gallantry, clicking his heels and bowing his head.

That moment was the payoff of our game. The drop of ink would run in an uneven violet stream along Ivan Alexandrovich's forehead, bewildering and frightening the person he was greeting.

Doubled up with laughter, we would rush to the bathroom, where we could safely break up laughing.

Ivan Alexandrovich considered me enemy number one. No matter who acted up in class, he would immediately pick on me.

"Worthless child! Pithecanthropus! Neanderthal!"

His rather impressive left fist would bang on my desk right under my nose, while the right hand, clutching the ruler, would be cautiously hidden behind his back. His sclerotic eyes, covered with thin red veins, would bulge behind thick, round, horn-rimmed glasses. Droplets of saliva would stick to his mustache, and spittle would bombard me. I would squint and even cover my face with the crook of my elbow. Jiggling on the Walrus's flabby old neck would be a black bow that he wore instead of a necktie. We used to joke that the former teacher from the tsarist Gymnasium did not remove the black bow because it was a sign of mourning for the dethroned Nicholas II.

"Ichthyosaurus! Brontosaurus! Neanderthal! Pithecanthropus! Don't show up at school tomorrow without your parents! Bring your father!" he yelled one day after I taunted him.

"How shall I bring him?" I asked innocently. "On a rope? Or a chain?"

The Walrus flapped his lips, his voice gone.

I got into the swing of things and to the amusement of the whole class went on: "My father can't come to school. He's a red commander and spends night and day strengthening the defenses of our country. How can he be torn away from such important work? Do you want to undermine the defenses of the USSR?"

"If your father can't come to school, then you'll have to leave the class. A punishment."

"It's not me you'll punish," I countered calmly, "but the Soviet government. Which is paying you to teach me and not keep me in the hallway."

"Silence!" Ivan Alexandrovich slammed his fist on the desk. His face and neck resembled an overripe tomato. "That's vile! It's out-and-out demagoguery! You'll grow up to be a fine executioner, a torturer! If you won't leave, I'll go!"

He quickly stuffed books into his bottomless briefcase, dropping them and picking them up from the floor, while a cleverly launched drop of ink settled into his hollow.

"Brontosaurus! Pithecanthropus!"

I saw the Walrus's red, wet mustache right before my eyes, and his round, horn-rimmed glasses staring at me. I discovered to my amazement that his glasses were missing one lens, so that on the left side, where there was a lens, his eye was magnified, and on the right, where the frame was empty, the eye was normal size.

"Worthless child." The Walrus was whispering for some reason. "Ichthyosaurus, Neanderthal . . ."

I unstuck my heavy eyelids and tried to focus, but I couldn't see our class behind the Walrus. All I saw behind his bald head was a square window with bars like ones I'd seen in movies about prisons.

"Ivan Alexandrovich," I whispered, "where is our class?"

"I don't know, lad." He blinked behind his one-lensed glasses. "We're far from home. In Orel . . . Do you remember that city? We studied it in geography."

"What are you doing here . . . in Orel?" I asked.

"Same as you . . . escaping from the Germans."

"Is this a prison?" I asked, still staring at the barred window.

"Yes," Ivan Alexandrovich said. "But it's empty. No prisoners . . . or guards. They've settled the refugees in here. . . . We found you here . . . with a fever. 'Look, Nadezhda Semyonovna,' I said to my wife, 'my Neanderthal is lying here in a fever.' 'Come on, Ivan Alexandrovich,' she replied, 'how could the child get so far from home all alone?' I was right! Pithecanthropus, ichthyosaurus . . . lying there, burning hot, doesn't even recognize his teacher. Where are your parents, vile child?"

"I don't know."

"Don't pester the child. He can barely breathe." His wife pushed the Walrus from my field of vision and appeared. She was a long-nosed, gray-haired woman I had never seen before. "He needs to take his medicine. Can you swallow one spoonful, dear? The military gave us this medicine for you."

"Is it bitter?" I sobbed, like a baby.

"Silence!" Ivan Alexandrovich roared. "Be a man, pithecanthropus! This is war. You have to follow orders."

"Stop it," Nadezhda Semyonovna said, and grimaced, as if she were the one who was about to swallow the medicine. She brought the wobbling spoon to my dry lips. I swallowed obediently and didn't even taste the yellow liquid.

"Bravo, brontosaurus," the Walrus said from behind his wife's back.

I shut my eyes.

"I think he's passing out again," Nadezhda Semyonovna said.

"We won't let him," Ivan Alexandrovich said confidently. I felt his tobacco breath on my face. "We're going to take a sea voyage from London to Sydney. I remember he knew that route rather well. And I hope he hasn't forgotten it."

I smiled and opened my eyes.

58

Several times the school's administration had tried to fire Ivan Alexandrovich, for the curses he heaped on the students and because he did not maintain discipline in his classes. And every time he was saved by his tormentors—us. We would send a delegation to the director and ask that he be kept on. If our pleas were not effective, we begged our parents to fight for the old teacher called Walrus.

We defended Walrus not only because he let us do headstands in his classes but because he taught us brontosauruses and Neanderthals to love geography. Our whole class, even the most delinquent *D* students, knew the globe by heart and could locate any point in the world even in our sleep. And not only find it, but relate in great detail what people lived there, what their customs were, what was manufactured there, and what mineral wealth was hidden in its bowels.

Our hearts trembling with delight, we would watch our short, mustachioed Walrus, his back to the map of both hemispheres, holding a pointer as large as a pool cue in both hands, and singing rapturously, like a nightingale, an ode to some seemingly uninteresting dot on the globe. And you would think that it was exactly that dot that the Walrus loved more than any other place in the world. We followed him, falling in love with Zanzibar, the Kalahari Desert, snowy Alaska, the Cape of Good Hope.

Without urging, we read everything we could get our hands on in the library about the great travelers, the discoverers of new lands, about the lives of people in different countries. Getting together after school, we would show off our store of facts to each other with the same passion with which we showed off our muscles and the ability to spit through our teeth farther than anyone else.

The best thing was being able to stand with your back to the map, not looking at it, and travel from one point to another, naming all the ports of call—the bays and sounds of the seas we sailed on, the islands and peninsulas we went around. It was the height of cool, casually, ever so matter-of-factly, to throw in some interesting details that were not in the school textbooks: "Our snow-white ship leaves the Moskva River Station and sails along the Moskva River to the first lock of the Moskva-Volga Canal, which connects the great Russian river, the Volga, with Moscow, the capital of our Homeland. Going from one lock to the next, our ship rises higher and higher, and then, crossing the Valdai Plateau, comes down to the Volga. We sail past ancient Russian cities . . . Murom . . . Uglich. . . . Uglich is famous in Russian history as the site where the underage tsarevitch Dmitri was killed in the days of Boris Godunov and the Polish pretender took the throne in his name—the adventurer Grishka Otrepev, called the False Dmitri among the folk. . . ."

And this was followed by an amusing story about the white ship sailing down the Volga; the ancient cities that lie on the banks of the river; the legendary rebel Stenka Razin, who attacked estates along the Volga and was later beheaded in Moscow on Red Square; about the Volga's delta, where migratory birds winter in the marshes and where precious red fish breed—salmon and beluga, which are not only tasty on their own, but are especially valued for their black caviar.

When I was called to the board, the Walrus would not look at me, but would turn to the window to hide his satisfaction. It so happened that I, his main enemy, was best at geography and traveled all over the globe without looking at the map or making mistakes.

I would see his knobby ears turn pink with pleasure, and his bald head nod in agreement, and when I was done, he would stamp over to his desk without looking at me and put a thick *B* in the class marking book. He never gave me an *A*.

"A Neanderthal can't be given the highest grade," he would say. "That would be a sign of disrespect for the *A*. The most gifted ichthyosaurus cannot achieve that grade. Even if his forehead were seven times bigger."

And now, in a godforsaken empty prison in Orel, where homeless evacuees had been settled, the Walrus was trying to call me back to life, to keep me from sinking into the haze of unconsciousness. He played on my vanity. Through my semicoma, with ears that seemed stuffed with cotton, I could hear his cracked, encouraging voice.

"It would please me if you would recall the route from London to Sydney. I don't think there was anyone in your class who was better at sea voyages."

"Leave the child alone," Nadezhda Semyonovna grumbled.

"Silence," the Walrus said angrily. "Please do not interfere. Sea voyages are not for ladies. Only we men are capable of traveling that far. Right, brontosaurus?"

I nodded, from nonbeing, from the other world.

And I strained myself to the limit to keep from losing Ivan Alexandrovich's hoarse voice, as if that voice were the last thread connecting me to the world.

"So, our ship leaves from the wall of the London dock," Ivan Alexandrovich whispered in my ear, and his walrus moustache tickled my cheek like a paintbrush. "A well-known Neanderthal is on deck. Where is he headed, eh?"

"To Sydney," I managed to breathe.

"To Sydney?" Ivan Alexandrovich was amazed. "So far? . . . How will you get there, what seas and oceans will you take?"

I took a few deep breaths and my head began to clear.

"We will sail down the Thames. . . ."

"Right, worthless child," my teacher said happily. "And then what, do you remember?"

With a flutter of my eyelashes I showed that I remembered, and licking my chapped lips with my swollen tongue, I said very softly: "From the mouth of the Thames we turn first southward, then west, into the Strait of Dover and the English Channel. We come out in the Bay of Biscay."

"Which is famous for its . . ." the Walrus prompted.

"Storms. . . . That's why they say those places roar with forty mouths. . . ."

"Bravo, pithecanthropus," the Walrus said, beaming. "We've weathered the storm, even though we're down in our berth with seasickness. . . . You're still pale. . . . But it happens . . . even to experienced sea wolves. . . ."

"You'll exhaust the child," Nadezhda Semyonovna,

whom I couldn't see, said indignantly. "Leave him alone."

"Please do not interrupt," the Walrus cut her off. "You, respected lady, might spoil our entire trip. So, brontosaurus, where are we now?"

"At Gibraltar."

"Absolutely correct."

"We are going through a narrow passage . . . into the Mediterranean . . . and heading east, to the Suez Canal. . . ."

"Oh, don't rush. We still have a long way to the Mediterranean. What is on our port side?"

"Port side?" I tried to remember. "First the shores of Spain . . . then France . . . Sardinia . . . Sicily."

"Now you are close to the shores of Africa? What's there?"

"Libya."

"Correct. That's on the starboard side. And on port we pass a tiny island. . . ."

"Malta," I sigh. "The main city and port of Malta is Valletta."

"Excellent!" Ivan Alexandrovich roared in my ear. "Nadya, this brontosaur knows more than today's admirals. He has a clear memory. Consequently, tomorrow, well, at worst, day after tomorrow, he will be completely well and will shame my gray hair with his terrible behavior."

"You have no gray hair," his wife rebuked him. "You're bald."

"Consequently, he'll shame *your* gray hair. In any case, we will not avoid shame from this worthless child."

And here I clearly heard a bird sing. Not outside, beyond the window, but right in the cell, behind my head, an unseen bird warbling.

"A bird?" I asked in amazement.

Nadezhda Semyonovna nodded.

"A canary."

"Where's the canary?"

"With us, child. We brought it from home."

She moved away for a second and returned, holding a small rounded cage of fine wire. A small yellow bird sat on a perch and turned its tiny head, trying to get a look at me.

"His name is Philip," Nadezhda Semyonovna said. "He's very very old. I couldn't leave him behind. So many years together . . . I will leave behind some of my things, but I won't leave Philip, I said to Ivan Alexandrovich. He argued, and argued, and gave in."

"Who can argue with you?" the Walrus said.

One of the others I couldn't see in the cell said grumpily: "People are losing their lives, Russia is in ruins, and she's worried about her canary."

"Don't you dare insult a lady." The Walrus leaped up, and his red mustache quivered angrily. "We have a right to be evacuated with Philip. He's part of the family. . . ."

The canary joined the fray, whistling and singing, and silence fell on the room, everyone listening to the bird, and someone was touched enough to whisper, "God's little bird."

"Why argue?" Nadezhda Semyonovna said to someone. "People should be cooperative in misfortune. Sit down, Ivan Alexandrovich, remember your heart."

He sat down next to me, removed his glasses, and wiped the solitary lens with his handkerchief. Without his glasses he no longer looked like a walrus, but like the great Ukranian poet Taras Shevchenko.

"Where's the other lens?" I asked.

"The other one?" Ivan Alexandrovich frowned. "The war took it. It's the sacrifice I made to Mars, the god of war. A crushed lens. If you don't count a few other things, like the house we lost, or our son, of whom there is no news. Only God knows whether he's alive. . . ."

"Be quiet," Nadezhda Semyonovna exclaimed. "You'll bring us bad luck. Why don't you go down to the pharmacy for medicine instead of wagging your tongue?"

And as he headed for the door with his worn corduroy jacket on his stooped shoulders, his wife anxiously called after him: "Watch you don't get lost."

Ivan Alexandrovich turned sharply, and his face and bald pate turned red.

"A teacher of geography, dear lady, who has the entire world in his head, cannot get lost in a pathetic provincial town. Brontosaurus, in my absence, please explain that to my wife."

The Walrus was away an hour. Then another. Nadezhda Semyonovna began worrying out loud and nervously pacing the room. Yellow Philip turned his head as he watched her from his cage.

"There's only one pharmacy in the whole city. It's

so far away. I'm afraid his heart gave out and he's died."

She was weeping, unembarrassed by my presence, when the door was flung open by a swift kick, and a Red Army man with a rifle came in and asked loudly:

"Is this old man yours?"

A shame-faced Walrus appeared in the doorway.

The soldier chewed him out as he left.

"Next time, pops, don't go into town alone. The patrols have better things to do than bring you home."

As soon as the soldier left, the Walrus straightened his shoulders and took a vial of medicine from his pocket.

"Never mind. Tomorrow you'll be fine."

I didn't get up on my own feet tomorrow, or even the next day. The crisis apparently was passing, but I was weaker than I could ever remember. I tried to get up from the plank bed and straw mattress but couldn't even sit up: I fell flat on my face and passed out from the exertion. Nadezhda Semyonovna brought me back to my senses with smelling salts that almost choked me. The smell made the canary sneeze. Ivan Alexandrovich ordered me to stay in bed without stirring.

Orel was bombed every day—the primary target of the German bomber planes was the railroad station. The transit prison, now stuffed with refugees like herring in a barrel, was only two hundred yards away. And I was one of the herring, flat on my back, staring at the ceiling, above which the sky crackled with exploding shells from the antiaircraft guns. My ears caught the steady hum of the German planes, the mounting whistle of the falling bomb. After that my ears didn't catch anything, because they were deafened by the thunder of a nearby explosion—and so my eyes took over: I saw the thick stone walls shake and drop a dusting of gray plaster onto my blanket. A hot wave of air rushed in through the paneless windows and tore my blanket off.

All the other refugees who lived in the prison cells jumped up from their plank beds at the first sound of the siren, abandoned their things, and ran like a stampeding herd into the hall and down the stairs to the cellar, deep underground, where the solitary confinement cells were. There, behind the thick concrete ceilings, you could survive even a direct hit on the prison.

But not me. And not Philip the canary, who ruffled his yellow feathers in fright. And not the two terrified old people who sat next to me. They couldn't lift me—they were too weak. So we four, left all alone in the empty prison, huddled close every time we heard the wail of a falling bomb and then relaxed when the explosion blasted hot air at us from the window, letting us know that it was all right for now, we had to wait and see what would happen next. And next was another wail, even fiercer and closer, seemingly right over our heads, and both fell upon me, wanting to cover me with their own bodies.

Ivan Alexandrovich and Nadezhda Semyonovna were covered with plaster. The gray dust lay on his eyebrows and mustache and on her nose and sharp chin. The canary in its cage was also changed from yellow to concrete gray.

The Walrus shook himself, just like a dog out of the

water, and spat out a clump of dust, raising a clenched fist at the ceiling, where plaster was still falling from the cracks.

"Neanderthals! Pithecanthropi!" he shouted hoarsely. "Bombing peaceful civilians! Eh? How about that? It's hard to believe that these degenerates are from the same race that gave the world Beethoven and Goethe."

The spiraling whistle of the next bomb cut off his eloquence. He grabbed Nadezhda Semyonovna and held her close. Then both old people huddled up to me, covering my body with theirs.

I spent a week in bed before I could finally get up unassisted. We were bombed every day, and the old couple never went to the shelter. They spent the air raids with me, and to our great luck there was never a direct hit on the prison. But the station was destroyed. Twice we were given the opportunity to leave Orel in an echelon of evacuees, but the old couple stayed with me. They were afraid that I would get chilled in the freight cars and become sicker.

By the time I was well enough to run around the deserted prison, the last wave of refugees was gone. There were no more trains out of Orel. The German tanks were approaching the city, and the remaining population was moving east on foot, carrying whatever they could.

The three of us had nothing. I hadn't had anything in the first place. Ivan Alexandrovich did have a tightly stuffed knapsack on his back, and Nadezhda Semyonovna carried Philip.

The city was in flames. Black smoke lay heavily over

the low wooden houses of the suburbs. Plank fences burned hot. Cracking and setting off showers of sparks, sunflowers burst into flames like candles, and then, their stalks broken, smoldered on soft garden soil. A small plywood birdhouse blazed in a burning tree and a starling whirled around it, crying in the blue-gray haze. We walked—I was in front, so that the old couple would not lose sight of me.

We spent the first night in a shed on freshly mowed, sweet-smelling hay. A cow breathed cozily in her stall and crickets chirped their song. The place smelled peacefully of milk and manure. I didn't want to think about the next day, which we would have to spend on the unprotected roads filled with tired, frightened people.

I sank into the hay and almost believed that I had no legs—I couldn't feel them for the exhaustion. But Nadezhda Semyonovna would not let me go to sleep without washing. Poking me in the back, she led me to the village well, sat me down on a damp bench, and then pulled up a bucket of water. She made me wash from the waist up and then scrub and rinse the dust from my feet. Only then did she allow me to go back to the haystack, shivering and covered with goose bumps.

The old people put me between them, spreading out Ivan Alexandrovich's corduroy jacket under me so the hay wouldn't stick me. He breathed noisily in the darkness, and the old woman lay quiet, as if she had stopped breathing.

"I want a story," I asked.

"What sissy nonsense," the Walrus sniffed. "Go to

sleep, brontosaurus. We're setting out early in the morning."

"I can't fall asleep without a story. Mama always told me a story at bedtime," I lied.

I knew from the movies that mothers told bedtime stories.

"Lord, don't torture the child," Nadezhda Semyonovna exclaimed. "Your tongue won't fall off from telling a story."

"A sto-ory," I whined like a baby. This was probably the first time, under the care of these people, that I felt like a child, and, weakened by my illness, I became whiny and demanding.

"What should I tell this ichthyosaur?" Ivan Alexandrovich drawled thoughtfully.

Nadezhda Semyonovna did not miss an opportunity for a jab.

"You're always talking nonstop, and now, when you need to . . ."

"A story must have a moral," Ivan Alexandrovich said. "A lesson for a good lad. So listen, you worthless child, and remember. Maybe you'll learn something. There was a young man . . ."

"Once upon a time," I corrected him.

"Absolutely correct. Once upon a time, in the fair city of Saint Petersburg, the capital of the Russian Empire, there lived a young man, and his name was Ivan. Of course, he wasn't a peasant lad: He came from an ancient noble line that began long ago in the times of Prince Dmitri Donskoi."

"The one who beat the Tatars on Kulikovo Field?" I interrupted.

70

"Absolutely correct. Nadya, I like this brontosaur more and more. . . . I see the fruits of my labor. Strangely enough, a few things stuck in the Neanderthal's brain."

The quiet hum of airplanes, growing louder, came over the shed roof.

"They're not going to bomb at night, too, are they?" Nadezhda Semyonovna asked anxiously.

"Not us," the Walrus said firmly. "We're no target for them. We're like gnats. They're headed for Moscow."

"Oh God, oh God," Nadezhda Semyonovna sobbed. "They won't stop even at night . . . even at night."

"Go on," I interrupted impatiently. "What happened next?"

"What could be next? As has been the custom since ancient times in noble families, when Ivan grew up, they sent him into the tsar's service. In the Life Guards Hussar regiment, in which Ivan's father, grandfather, and great-grandfather had served impeccably before him."

"Wow!" I said.

"Life smiled upon Ivan," the Walrus mumbled over my ear. "He was young, handsome, rich. He handled the service easily, playfully. Ahead of him—marriage to a woman from his own circle of noble and wealthy people, children to continue the famous line, and an easy, carefree life, filled with joy and pleasure. But fate had other things in store for him."

"The Revolution?" I guessed.

"No. This happened before the Revolution," the

Walrus said. "Love happened to Ivan. The regiment was stationed in a small town, in Polesie, inside the Pale of Settlement."

"What is the Pale of Settlement?" I asked.

"Thank God, child, that you don't know," Nadezhda Semyonovna sighed to me.

"But as a historical fact it is good for him to know," Ivan Alexandrovich insisted. "The Pale of Settlement was a place in the western part of the Russian Empire where Jews were permitted to live. Like a large ghetto that incorporated many provinces of the Ukraine, Belorussia, Poland, and Lithuania. Jews were not allowed to live in other places. For instance, in Saint Petersburg and Moscow, along the Volga, and so on, to the east."

"Why not?"

"Don't break your head with these problems, child," Nadezhda Semyonovna said. "Thank goodness, the Revolution put an end to that."

"And gave rise to new problems," Ivan Alexandrovich said, "worse than the old ones. But we're not talking about that. I'm telling a story. Let them deal with politics in the Kremlin."

"Ivan fell in love," I prodded him.

"Absolutely correct. Madly in love, fatally, with a girl from a very poor family, a Jewish girl at that. A mésalliance! A scandal! Flouting all the conventional norms of decency. Ivan's mother was in a faint. His father was enraged. His fellow hussars considered him mad. It was the end of a brilliant career. His prospects were joyless poverty and total isolation. Society did not forgive such escapades."

72

The Walrus breathed heavily and moved about in the hay with a crunch.

"What happened?" I couldn't stand the suspense.

"The usual banal story. The hussar abducted the girl and they went off. Farewell, regiment! Farewell, former life! Hello, love! Isn't there an old saying that even a tent is paradise when you're with your beloved? It's true if your tent actually happens to be in paradise."

"Ivan Alexandrovich, cynicism doesn't suit you," Nadezhda Semyonovna told him sharply, and then whispered in my ear.

"Listen to him selectively, child, don't take everything for gospel."

The Walrus went on. "There were many obstacles in the path of the lovers. Her family in that little town disowned her and mourned her in the synagogue as if she were dead. Because in order to marry Ivan, the Jewish girl had to give up her Jewish faith for the Christian Orthodox faith of her beloved and marry him in a church.

"Ivan even had to shed blood for his love. He challenged a hussar officer who was disrespectful about Ivan's beloved to a duel and was shot in the chest, and it was only his wife's tender loving hands that brought him back to life.

"They settled far from her little town and from his Petersburg and began living the hard life of labor, for Ivan had been stripped of his capital and inheritance.

"Then came the Revolution. The plebeians and proletarians came to power. But they did not consider Ivan one of their own. They deprived him of all rights

73

because he was a former nobleman. And if it hadn't been for his wife, whose proletarian heritage was indisputable, he would have been killed. But they didn't finish him off. They even graciously allowed him to earn his daily bread. And then . . ."

"And then I know what happened," I said sarcastically.

"Really?" the Walrus feigned surprise.

"Then came the war and they had to abandon their home and become refugees," I said, speaking as fast as I could. "And to their misfortune, in the city of Orel they came upon a worthless child, a brontosaur and Neanderthal. . . ."

"An incredibly smart ichthyosaur," the Walrus praised me. "And now you get to sleep, or we won't be able to wake you in the morning. Learn from what you heard. The story has a moral."

We left at dawn, feeding and milking the cow and setting her loose in the beet field. And we walked across the dewy beet tops to the road humming with vehicles and blended into the flow of refugees streaming nonstop to the east, away from the war.

By noon the sun was broiling, and Nadezhda Semyonovna grew ill. She dropped the bird cage and leaned on my shoulder, her head thrown back to the sky and her mouth open and quivering. Ivan Alexandrovich held her from the other side, and the two of us, struggling against the flow of dusty, sweaty people, dragged her to the side of the road and sat her on the edge of a dry ravine. I went back for the canary and set it on the grass. Yellow Philip, also slightly dazed by the heat, cocked his head in amazement at his mistress, who was lying on her back.

"I'll be a burden to you," Nadezhda Semyonovna whispered piteously, panting in short, shallow breaths.

"Silence!" Ivan Alexandrovich cried. "It does not befit your age to utter stupidities. You always had a weak heart. You'll lie down and rest and you'll feel better, and in the meantime I will stop a car and we will ride on."

He ran out into the road. Stubbornly, his head lowered like a bull, he pushed into the crowd, and I saw his corduroy jacket and black bow flickering amid the backs and heads.

"Kind people," came an unaccustomed pleading, ingratiating voice. "An old woman is sick. . . . She cannot walk. . . . She has to be taken to the nearest town. . . . Please, in the name of God. I beseech you."

People walked around Ivan Alexandrovich indifferently, and cars stuffed with belongings and with people hanging from the running boards drove past.

Ivan Alexandrovich's voice grew dimmer.

"Show some mercy. . . . Don't abandon us in our misfortune. . . . An old woman . . . my wife . . ."

No one had time for him, a bald old man in a corduroy jacket with a black bow around his neck. People were carrying children, helping old women, pushing carts with suitcases and bundles. They seemed aloof, and I thought that the suffering they were going through had made them deaf and that the only thing they could hear was their own footsteps.

"I'm better now," Nadezhda Semyonovna said, when a depressed Ivan Alexandrovich returned and sat down next to her, frowning. "I'll rest just a bit more and we can go on."

And soon we did go on, she in the middle, we on either side. I carried the birdcage. Nadezhda Semyonovna rested one arm on her husband's shoulder and pressed down on my neck with the other, but I did not pay any attention to that and concentrated on moving my feet, feeling grown-up and proud that someone's life depended on my endurance.

Nadezhda Semyonovna gasped, and we stopped and sat down to rest. Ivan Alexandrovich gave her a pill and a sip of water from a flask.

And we went on.

The road led deep into a forest. The high crowns of fir trees rustled on both sides. Beneath them were large lacy ferns. The soft moss looked inviting. The forest called on us to rest, so we got off the dusty road onto the springy, soft moss pillows, and walked along them until we reached a sunny meadow. Nadezhda Semyonovna said, "It's so beautiful here."

She sank onto the moss as if it were a mattress, and the filigree ferns moved around her, letting through nothing but dappled bits of sunlight.

The meadow charmed Philip too. He sang gently, and through the ferns I saw a smile touch Nadezhda Semyonovna's blue lips.

"God! How beautiful," she whispered. "Must I really . . . leave . . . this magical world?"

"Nonsense," Ivan Alexandrovich replied. "I heard a cow moo. The village, as I figure it, is that way.

Judging by the moss on the tree trunks, south is that way, and north, consequently in the opposite direction. I will head southwest, and ergo I will get help. I'll be back soon."

And he set off, but his wife's weak voice stopped him.

"Vanya," she called softly, and when he returned and bent over her, she whispered, "Kiss me."

"What inappropriate sentiments," Ivan Alexandrovich grumbled, looking over guiltily at me. He removed his glasses and plunged his head into the ferns.

He left, and I listened for a long time to the crackle of twigs under his boots, and then even those noises melted into the light rustle of the trees above my head. Philip grew still and sat hunched on his perch.

"I feel better, I think," Nadezhda Semyonovna said. "I'll sleep a bit. I'm afraid you'll have to wait for Ivan Alexandrovich to return alone, child."

I sat among the ferns with my back to her and listened to her breathing: fast and shallow, as if she were drinking the air like freezing ice water, with tiny sips.

I did not know how much time had passed since Ivan Alexandrovich had gone, but according to my calculations, it was time for him to be back. It would be dark soon, and then he would never find the way back.

I peered into the depths of the woods, pricked up my ears for snapping twigs, and suddenly I realized: Nadezhda Semyonovna's shallow breathing was no longer coming from the ferns. A fuzzy bumblebee buzzed, treading air.

I crawled over and pushed the ferns aside with my

head and shoulders. Nadezhda Semyonovna seemed to be sleeping, her eyes shut, her mouth open. But she wasn't breathing. Her chest was still.

"Are you asleep?" I asked with a quaver in my throat.

She did not hear. Then I nudged her shoulder. She did not move.

"Nadezhda Semyonovna!" I called.

Still no answer.

The horrible realization had already reached my brain, but I chased it away, unwilling to take it on faith. I remembered that in such cases people check the pulse, feeling around somewhere on the wrist. I took her hand and immediately pulled mine away, as if I had been hit by electricity. Her hand was cold.

The bumblebee buzzed over her pointed nose.

There was no doubt about it. She had died. Quietly, in her sleep. I hadn't even noticed. I looked around in fear. My eyes found a living creature—the yellow canary in the wire cage next to the gray head of his mistress. The canary blinked his canary eyes, as if asking me if it were true.

"She's dead," I whispered.

And the canary whistled softly, cocking his head toward the dead face. Then again. He seemed to expect her to respond. And not getting a response, he warbled a long trill. So bitter and sad, I thought: This is how canaries weep. Then I wept too.

I was sobbing and howling, the way a wolf cub must howl lost from his pack and left alone in the woods. The sad song of the tiny yellow bird hovered over my shoulder, mourning the dead.

I began calling, "Ivan Alexandrovich! Ivan Alexandrovich!"

I listened. Nothing.

I ran, far from the corpse, in the direction my teacher had taken. I ran looking for him, to tell him the terrible news and to bring him to the place where his wife lay.

The moss sank under my feet and I stumbled. I fell on my knees, scraping them badly on branches that stuck out from the moss. And ran again. Gasping, swallowing the thick pine-resiny air. I was lost. Ivan Alexandrovich was probably wandering around too. I began shouting, calling him. This time I heard a response, but it was a stranger's voice. A bearded man with a horsewhip in his hand came out from behind the trees.

"What are you shouting about? Are you lost?"

Sobbing, I started telling him about Nadezhda Semyonovna, and he interrupted:

"What's she to you, a granny?"

I nodded.

"Well, may she rest in peace."

He shifted the whip to his left hand, removed his hat, and crossed himself with sweeping movements, as if chasing mosquitoes.

"Lucky I was passing by," he said, pulling on his hat. "Come with me."

"What about Grandma?"

"What can happen to your grandma? She's in heaven now. The angels are taking care of her."

He brought me in total darkness to the village. I didn't go to bed until I had checked with all the neighbors, asking if they had seen an old man, bald and with a mustache. Everyone responded negatively.

In the morning the man went back to the woods with me. We wandered a long time until we found the fern-covered meadow. It was bright and sunny, and the yellow canary was singing in the wire cage. Nadezhda Semyonovna lay in the same position, but now drops of dew glistened in her gray hair.

She was buried in the village cemetery. I was asked her religion, and I was about to say Jewish, but I remembered the hussar who took his bride away from the village and married her in a church, and said that she was Russian Orthodox. Over her grave they placed a cross, knocked together out of two unplaned planks.

Ivan Alexandrovich never showed up. I waited for him for three days and then went away. I left the yellow canary in the man's house. He gave me a honeycomb for the road.

Part II

4

The enormous multitiered crystal chandelier blazed with thousands of sparks right before our eyes. We were seated in the first row of the balcony, leaning on the worn raspberry velvet of the rounded barrier. In the orchestra seats bald heads glinted, officers' shoulder boards gleamed gold, and the colorful hairdos of the women swayed like dandelions.

We were in luck—we had the entire center from aisle to aisle. All the seats were filled by our group, like starlings on a fence: in black shirts, black cotton trousers, hair slicked back with water but popping up in cowlicks when it dried. Foreman Kostenko sat right in the middle of the row and turned his small head with its round owlish eyes sternly and anxiously. He did not believe our vows to behave in the theater like decent people, and his right arm, crippled at the front and permanently shaped into a red, bony fist, hung menacingly from the barrier. Each of us had encountered that fist.

Our gang, which is the only thing Foreman Kostenko ever called us, unexpectedly received the nicest surprise: a trip to the theater. Why? We never knew. Our work was no better and no worse than before. The foreman said that it wasn't for us to figure out, the administration knew what it was doing, and all we had to do was say thank you and go to the theater in an organized and disciplined way—and there had better be no incidents on the way there or back or at the theater. To be more convincing he brandished his stump under our wet, runny noses.

"The theater is a temple. Understand?" Foreman Kostenko explained to us. "Everything there is delicate and cultured. If it were up to me, I wouldn't let you thieves and bandits in there in a month of Sundays. It is strictly forbidden in the theater to spit from the balcony on the heads of people below, and also to foul the air or swear out loud. So, I repeat, the theater is a temple. And whoever steals from a temple is a Judas!"

Out of our entire group only I had any relation to Judas and his tribe—I was the only Jew. Nevertheless, I hotly promised the foreman along with the rest of the group that we would not let him down and he would not have to call us Judases.

We walked from the factory to the station in two black lines grinning from ear to ear, intoxicated by the burning frosty air, anticipating a whole day off from work, without soot and rats. Our bloodless sunken cheeks grew rosy, our eyes began to glisten, and like ice melting, we turned from big-headed dwarves into normal children.

We swallowed the delicious air with our open mouths and like horses exhaled billows of steam.

A stuffed sack bounced on Foreman Kostenko's back. It held our daily food allowance, distributed as dry rations: slices of black bread and a small bag of granulated sugar. We had breakfasted hurriedly in the factory canteen—the food merely whetted the hunger that was always gnawing at us. We couldn't take our eyes off the food bag on his back, and our mouths watered so much that we kept spitting into the snow.

The small railroad station in the Urals, where we caught a train to Sverdlovsk, provided temptation hard to resist. The station was paradise for hungry thieves. Passengers crowded along the platform waiting for the train, and many had knapsacks on their backs. Even without touching, just with our eyes, we could tell where homemade rye crackers, prepared for the long journey, pushed against the fabric of the packs.

So many times our boys had gone over to the station, blending into the crowd, each finding a man, then pressing up against him, crisscrossing his pack with a sharp razor blade, and taking the crisp toasted crackers. They didn't fall on the ground, but into a waiting cap. And when the cap was overflowing, you just had to move a bit and elbow your way out.

And here were crowds of peasant men on the platform, their backpacks bursting with homemade crackers. We could hear them crackle as we pressed against them. But we kept our hands in our pockets, and our razor blades chilled the tips of our fingers uselessly. Foreman Kostenko, taller than us by a head, glanced left and right suspiciously, and we ducked our heads into the raised collars of our coats and angrily spat at the ground and the men's boots. Were we to open even one sack, we'd never see the theater. Foreman Kostenko would herd us back home.

When the train came, Vanya Burmistrov, called Pelican, pushed aside the peasant men and was first into the car, where he opened the windows so that we could climb in, helping one another, and take over half the seats, even saving a place for Foreman Kostenko by stretching out our legs. He came in last, calmly, without shoving, and sat down, wiping away the wet snow our boots had left on the seat. And the train, as if it had been waiting for him, sounded its horn and took off. Past the windows, thawed by our breath, rolled cliffs and pines, then at the turn we saw the familiar brick smokestacks of our factory. We even tried to pick out our shop, but couldn't. From a distance, they all looked alike—sooty.

The master put his food sack on his lap, untied it without rushing, dipped into it with his good left hand, and pulled out the first packet. Four slices of soggy, sticky black bread, with stubs of bran bristling from the damp interior. Then he placed a tiny paper bag of sugar on the bread and ordered us to pass it along to the farthest kids. So our packets began traveling from hand to hand through the car, and as soon as a kid got his ration, he first poured the sugar into his mouth, and then took a bite of the bread and smacked it so loudly that it could be heard throughout the car. I unwrapped my paper bag and dunked the soggy bread into the pile of sugar. When I bit in, my cheeks puckered and felt tingly, as if there were acid in my mouth instead of saliva.

We were like animals. We gulped down our rations for the day greedily and hurriedly.

The peasant men standing in the aisle lit up their home-grown shag tobacco to keep from thinking about food, and acrid smoke filled up the car.

"Stop that smoking!" Foreman Kostenko bawled like a sergeant. "Can't you see the children eating?"

The children—that was us. That was the first time the foreman had ever referred to us as that. Usually, when he was yelling at us, he called us peasants, clods, and parasites who should be at the front, fighting for victory and not hiding in the rear.

The men quickly tossed their handrolled cigarettes to the floor and stamped them out.

We rejoiced, but not for long. The soggy underdone bread and the pile of sugar swallowed without chewing brought on stomach cramps. We were bloated, full of gas. But remembering the foreman's orders not to pass gas in public, we held it in as best we could, grimacing and writhing. The sounds of our stomachs growling sounded like a dozen heated frying pans cooking bacon at the same time.

Foreman Kostenko frowned and twitched his nostrils and perked up his ears, hoping to catch a perpetrator and cancel the trip to the theater.

The stomach grumbling continued even when we took our seats in the first row of the balcony. From below rose the thick and strong reek of cheap wartime perfume and cosmetics. The women were skinny and bony, and their dresses were remodeled from years ago. The men were all in green camouflage outfits, young officers in new uniforms with creaking leather straps and old bald men, to whom even a military uniform couldn't give a brave and sharp air. There were almost no middle-aged men, and I realized that that whole generation had been wiped out by the war. My father was also middle-aged.

Our row stared at the dressy orchestra seats, inhaling the unfamiliar, exciting scents that came from that other, distant world. By the way their lips moved and jaw muscles worked, I could tell how hard it was for my pals to resist the temptation to spit at such enticing targets as a gleaming bald head or a bleached hairdo. Only the fear of missing a rare experience like the theater kept us within the framework of decency.

We were going to see a performance of Konstantin Simonov's extremely popular play *Wait for Me*. The whole country knew his poem of the same name, and even we, not quite grown up yet, could recite it with feeling:

> Wait for me, and I'll return.
> But wait very hard.

It wasn't even a poem but a prayer, from a soldier to his wife or sweetheart, left behind. He called on her to be true to him and not lose hope of meeting again, and then he truly would not die but survive in spite of death.

On one condition: "But wait very hard."

That was very easy to understand for us. In our code of honor, loyalty was one of the most important things. We understood what separation was. We were all terribly lonely, without families or relatives, without warmth and tenderness. Therefore it was easy for us to get into the skin of that soldier, who suffered with deep longing. To be disloyal to him seemed a pitiless, horrible crime without any justification or excuse. And our hearts stopped when we heard the line of the desperate request:

But wait very hard.

The dark burgundy curtain moved, wrinkled up into vertical folds, and floated off to the sides, revealing the interior of an urban apartment. The action began. We, who had forgotten furniture, curtains on windows, and shades on lamps, who had forgotten the coziness of home life, stared at that ordinary apartment as at a miracle. Because we slept on wooden cots, ate at bare tables, and had rough-hewn stools for chairs. The stage smelled of home, parental warmth, and we gaped until intermission.

We followed the course of the play with bated breath. A beautiful woman waited for news from the front about a handsome pilot. She was told that he was killed, but she didn't believe it and kept on waiting. The audience knew that he was alive, shot down over enemy territory. It was taking many days and many nights to get back to her. Everyone told her that he was dead, that there was no point in waiting, but she stubbornly waited and came out in front of the curtain right to the footlights and told not the whole audience, not those bald officers and their painted ladies, but told us, our row in the balcony, with great feeling and controlled tears, that she would wait no matter what.

The curtain floated out from both sides to the center and hid her. And the audience broke out in stormy applause. We clapped the loudest, till our hands hurt, with hot faces and swollen eyes. Our whole gang fell for her like a ton of bricks, and we all glowed in the light of the chandelier as if we had performed some heroic deed ourselves.

"Easy, easy," Foreman Kostenko whispered angrily, as we headed for the lobby. "Don't take it so seriously."

The audience strolled around in the lobby, and we wandered around in a black little bunch, subdued by our emotions, avoiding one another's suspiciously damp eyes.

That stroll was hard for us. They were selling ice cream in the lobby. We hadn't seen ice cream since before the war. And here they were selling it. It wasn't the prewar kind, but made with saccharine. But it was still ice cream.

Our hearts froze. Ice cream was expensive. And we didn't have any money.

The servicemen were buying it for their ladies, though. They had enough money in their plump wallets, which carelessly peeked out of their pockets and just begged to be plucked. Our fingers itched and our palms sweated. But no one swiped a wallet—because then Kostenko . . .

We stared at the ice cream in the ladies' fingers, at the ladies' tongues licking it, and the ladies' noses crinkling because the ice cream wasn't as good as it had been before the war.

We swallowed the saliva from our watering mouths and looked where we could spit, because you don't spit on the floor in the theater.

Then the bell rang and everyone headed back into the theater, and we went up to the balcony. By the time we found our seats and the curtain began moving, we forgot all about the ice cream and were all enraptured with the play.

A friend of the husband returned from the front and told the woman that he himself saw her husband die. This friend had been in love with her for a long time and now asked her to marry him. She wept and wrung her hands, paced the stage, and our hearts followed her around the stage. An ominous foreboding crept into our souls. Then came the moment we had anticipated with horror. She lowered her head on his shoulder, and he embraced her.

A deathly silence hung over the theater, like at a funeral. Our nerves were at the breaking point. Suddenly, like thunder, from the first row of the balcony came a weeping moan: "You bitch!"

It seemed to me that every crystal pendant of the dimmed chandelier trembled.

"Up!" barked Foreman Kostenko. "To the exit— march!"

Hunched over and cringing, we obediently rose and marched, eyes front, to the exit, accompanied by the disapproving hum of the shocked audience.

No one glanced back at the stage.

In two columns we were led down dark, icy Sverdlovsk to the train station. Foreman Kostenko maintained a furious silence. We were silent too, recovering from the shock. Occasionally, whispered curses fell from our lips.

At the station endless throngs of passengers bustled, waiting for the train. Many had packs on their backs, and the toasty rye smell tickled our nostrils. Our hands sought the razor blades in our pockets. The taut fabric of the sacks zipped open under our blades. The aromatic home-baked crackers fell crunching into our caps. Working our elbows furiously, we got out of the crowd, and we could hear the first cries of the peasant men who discovered that their packs suddenly felt very light.

With a rumble and a roar the train rolled up to the platform, wreathed in frosty steam.

Foreman Kostenko stood the whole way back in the corridor with the peasants. We sat. No one saved him a seat.

5

On New Year's Eve the moon shimmered over the Ural Mountains in a rainbow halo, and the snowy cliffs and coniferous forest creaked, as if cracking in the frost.

The day had been short. On New Year's Eve the factory worked only a half shift, but when our grimy-faced crowd came out at lunchtime, it was already dark, and lights glimmered dully throughout the factory grounds.

We were given a holiday lunch. For the first time in many weeks the tickling aroma of meat rose from our metal bowls. We were given one hamburger pattie each—horsemeat, stretched by bread. We knew that horse. Shaggy, stumpy legged, with a swollen belly, he couldn't work anymore. They had used him to haul an icy barrel of water from a hole in the river to the

93

kitchen. Lately they had to hold him up with straps to keep him from falling, and every time we passed the canteen we saw his dreary face and sad, filmed eyes through the stable door.

And then we all crowded into the dorm room, climbed into bed with our clothes on, and piled up our coats and quilted jackets on top of the blankets. Only our cold noses stuck out. Even though we had stoked up the stove with pine logs split into fine, oily kindling, the warmth quickly dissipated. We lay, seventeen boys, on wooden camp beds pushed close together, in fetal position, conserving what little warmth we had.

Even lunch with the horsemeat pattie wasn't enough to stave off our hunger. We never had enough to eat and we were always painfully hungry, twenty-four hours a day, even in our sleep.

The New Year brought memories of glowing decorated trees, presents, and lots and lots of candy. We had forgotten the taste of candy during the war.

We boys, pale to the point of blueness, were not intended to have New Year's trees, sparklers, or presents. We had been made part of the working class, we were considered adults. But among adults we looked like puny dwarves.

Our beds stood in three rows. We didn't want to move and we did not feel like talking. Someone, cursing, mad at himself, remembered before the war when he ate fried eggs cooked in bacon.

"Shut up, you viper!" we howled, swallowing hard. "Another word and we'll choke you!"

It grew quiet. Then someone else began:

"I remember for New Year's my Mama would . . ."

"What Mama? What are you lying for? You had shit, not a Mama!"

"What do you think, I was born in a orphanage or something?"

"No, like Jesus Christ, from the Holy Spirit."

"He didn't have a pappy, but he had a mammy. She gave him milk. . . ."

"What milk?"

"Warm . . ."

"Shut up, you!"

The mention of warm milk, to which my memory added a white roll, soft and springy, was more than I could stand.

"So this is it," Roman said. "Anyone else squawks about food, he gets a pool cue on the noggin. . . . Got it? Let's talk about something else. . . . Here, for instance, which of you bums could stand any kind of torture, but not reveal secrets to the fascists?"

We grew quiet as we pondered.

"What kind of torture?" someone asked meekly.

"Well, pulling your teeth out," Roman said. "And needles under your nails, red hot . . ."

His imagination could not go beyond that.

"Well, could you stand it?"

"Why not? I could, if I'd had a good meal before."

And he bit his tongue, remembering Roman's threat.

The conversation wasn't going well. Then Vanya Burmistrov from the far corner bed started singing softly and piteously like a beggar on the church steps about the convicts on Sakhalin, a song we all liked because we thought it was about us.

Vanya sang with an unsteady voice, and we listened, feeling sorry for ourselves.

> "No one pitied us.
> We suffered from scurvy.
> They gave us fish and water."

The tears formed. But we held on, sniffling hard.

Vanya held the notes and then took a deep breath and bitterly flung the next line at our chilled heads: "There are prostitutes there. . . ."

We didn't hear the rest. We wept out loud, wailing, choking on our sobs. Prostitutes seemed like the end of the world to us. You couldn't think of anything worse.

When he finished singing Vanya Burmistrov listened to our sobs like his earned applause and then, pleased with his success, began another song. About a tramp who ran from Sakhalin along a narrow animal track. And how he died in the taiga of Siberia, never having made it home, and his final words made our hearts ache as if we were the ones frozen in the snow instead of him, realizing that:

> My wife will find herself another
> But my mother will never find another son.

We pitied the poor old mother who would never be solaced so much that we forgot shame and wept.

When Vanya started a third song, I couldn't take it anymore. I pulled on the quilted jacket and then the coat and went out into the street.

The moon was frozen to the black sky and belted with pale circles. Above the dark log houses smoke rose straight up in thick columns from the chimneys.

I wandered in the creaking snow, my head tucked into my shoulders and my hands thrust deep in my pockets. I wandered wherever my feet took me, just so I wouldn't have to hear those howling sad songs.

My feet took me to the only illuminated windows. It was the local school. Through the frosted double windows I could hear the babble of children's voices and the sound of the concertina.

I peered through the glass but couldn't see anything through the frost, so I blew as hard as I could until the ice melted and I could make out vague outlines beyond the glass. I saw a New Year's tree, and toys glittering on it, and candles with their living tongues of flame.

Grandfather Frost stood by the tree wearing a white cotton beard, waving a red mitten as he conducted a song. The children sitting around the tree, singing and holding hands, were only a year or two younger than I, dressed in normal children's clothing, not in uniforms. These children didn't work at the factory. They had not lost their childhood. They had parents, and their fathers hadn't died at the front but were waiting for the end of the war deep in the rear, in the Urals.

For these kids, childhood continued. They danced underneath the tree, and Grandfather Frost handed out presents to them. They wore short pants and dresses, and the girls had ribbons in their hair. I was wearing a padded jacket stinking of metal cinders like dog flesh, a coat as black as death, and oversize yellow tarpaulin shoes stuffed with newspapers for warmth.

A very long time ago we had a tree like that in our house, and my mother invited the children of the officers in Father's division and dressed up as Grandfather Frost herself. Wearing shorts and with my ears scrubbed until they were red, I recited a poem, and they applauded not only because I read it well but also because I was the commander's son.

Now I was no longer a child and nobody's son. I was freezing in a snowdrift under the lighted window and swearing at those people indoors in a very adult way.

To warm up, I ran down the empty road, dodging the frozen clumps of horse manure. I reached the lake. Covered with ice and snow, it separated the village from the factory. Paths meandered over the ice and I ran down one of them. Stars radiated cold above me. The glimmering lights of the village receded. Ahead loomed the three smokestacks of the power station— three columns of blue-gray smoke held up the sky.

The lake was deserted. All living creatures were hidden in the warmth of heated houses, sitting around tables, looking at the clock. Soon the Moscow chimes would ring on the radio and strike twelve with a happy jingle. And the Moscow announcer, in his familiar, well-fed voice, would say, just as he had last year and the year before: "Happy New Year, comrades!"

Oh, how much food would be consumed immediately throughout the land of the Soviets. Impossible to imagine. Herring, sliced and layered with onion rings, pieces of bread slathered with butter, and crunchy green pickles. My mouth puckered just thinking about it. That had been happening a lot to me lately, when

I thought about food. But this was something else. In the frosty air, on the ice of the empty lake, my nostrils caught the weak aroma of baking bread. At first I thought I was dreaming and that hunger had driven me mad. But straining my eyes, I saw two dark figures headed toward me along the path. The bread aroma was coming from them. It was a boy and girl, probably brother and sister. The boy had a fur hat with ear flaps pulled down deep over his head, and the girl's head, shoulders, and back were covered by a warm wool scarf knotted tightly in the back. To his chest, the boy was hugging . . . a loaf of bread. He looked around twelve, just a bit younger than I. And the girl couldn't have been over ten.

They couldn't miss me on the narrow path. They were skipping toward me, slowing down as they drew near. They instinctively sensed danger in me.

They weren't mistaken. I wouldn't let them get around me. I grabbed the loaf from the boy, and now it was *my* arms that were pressing the bread to my chest.

The children didn't scream, and they didn't cry. Like wind-up toys, they hopped up and down clumsily in the crisp snow, and began whining, just like puppies.

"Mi-is-ter," they whimpered. "Give back the bread, mister."

At first I didn't understand whom they were talking to. There was no one on the lake except the three of us. And then I understood. They were calling me "mister." I was an adult to them. And I was barely older than the boy.

"Mis-ster," the children begged, hopping around me. "Give it ba-ack . . . or our mom will beat us. Mi-is-ter . . ."

And I gave it back, with unfeeling hands, not understanding why. I was so stunned by that "mister."

"Come on, git from here!" I shouted after them. They ran like crazy down the path and soon disappeared in the blue darkness.

I was alone again. I stood on the ice and spat in despair into the snow.

"Jerk!" I berated myself. "You could have broken off a chunk. You're a fool, not a mister!"

As I approached the dorm, it was getting on toward midnight. I didn't meet a single person. From the black loudspeaker on a post the Kremlin chimes from distant Moscow rang out. And the announcer called to my back: "Happy New Year, comrade!"

"Go———yourself!" I spat out.

Spring comes late to the Urals, and the deep snow that has lain on the ground all winter, and been forged by the frosts to a rocklike consistency, suddenly starts sinking beneath your feet and seeping moisture into the deep prints.

The cornices of the steep roof of our shop spouted flat icicles overnight, as thick as sticks with sharpened ends. The day before one had broken off and banged a Rumanian POW on the head. Many POWs worked in our shop: Germans, Rumanians, and Hungarians. With the onset of spring, they ran out of the stinking shop at lunch to warm up in the sunshine. The icicle killed the Rumanian on the spot. At least that's what they said later. For some time now death had become so customary that it did not arouse curiosity.

From the factory to the dorm I took a shortcut,

through a ravine filled with snow to the top. I sank in up to my waist. I wanted to turn back and take the long way, which was well traveled and trampled, when something caught my eye on the other side of the ravine: two dark figures fooling around. Obviously two of ours, guys from the shop, in their black coats. Then I saw that they weren't fooling around—they were fighting.

Looking hard, I recognized the combatants. Those boys lived in my room. One was called Ivan. The other was Syoma. They were both orphans practically from birth and had no idea what kind of families they had come from. The only thing known was that Ivan was Russian and Syoma Jewish. Syoma had the saddest eyes and a drooping nose much too large for his tiny face. They called Syoma "Tiny." He was the smallest and puniest in our team. All the boys except for me came from an orphanage in the Ukraine. They were evacuated to the Ural Mountains when the Germans advanced. Their backgrounds were similar—they lost their parents during the famine in the early thirties in the Ukraine, and they were picked up, blue and bloated, next to their parents' bodies and brought up on state food. What kind of food that was could be judged from their underdeveloped bodies and large heads on skinny necks. Ivan, for instance, was called "Rickets."

Rickets was beating up Tiny, shoving the boy's nose into the crumbly snow and kicking him in the ribs, and shouting so that even I could hear: "Kike! Kike! Take that! And that!"

I was also a Jew and knew that the word "kike" was

an insult to all Jews. I had never been called that filthy word in my life. And I was hearing it used as ammunition against a specific individual for the first time.

Sinking in the snow, I rushed to Tiny's aid, impelled by a newly aroused sense of religious solidarity.

Rickets saw me, and tried to get away, but he floundered in the snow and I caught up with him. I punched his snotty face a couple of times and kicked him in the butt. Whining and whimpering, he crawled out of the ravine. I went back to Tiny, sitting waist deep in snow. Guiltily, the sad eyes of Syoma Silberman regarded me—he was a boy who had not known parents, brothers, or sisters, but only his roommates in an orphanage, where everyone was stronger and picked on him constantly.

"Get up!" I ordered. "And don't be a coward! Never offer yourself like a sheep. I'll stick up for you if necessary."

"I won't go with you," Tiny said, his girlish eyelashes blinking fast. "They'll beat you."

"Who'll touch me?"

"What about Roman?" Tiny looked at me like a condemned man. "Rickets is his brother."

A chill ran under my coat. Rickets was considered Roman's brother. They had the same surname, and Rickets was Roman's protégé. And no one wanted to mess with Roman.

He had all the other fifteen inhabitants of our room under his thumb. They served him like slaves, giving him their meager rations and even their clothes when he felt like showing off. He didn't go to work—his quota was done by others. Our factory foreman, a quiet sickly man, told Roman when anyone needed disciplining, and Roman took care of the problem with an iron fist. He didn't do the beating himself; he didn't stoop to dirty work. Lolling on his cot, he commanded the execution. The victim was beaten up by a horde of hungry, mean boys under Roman's orders.

I was new here, and Roman, like a good dictator, crafty and treacherous, was in no hurry to extend his power over me. I wasn't an orphan and was strong and muscular and wasn't afraid of him. Everyone was a head shorter than me. Roman was no exception, but in contrast to the rest, he was big-boned.

In every vocational school in the Urals that I was brought to, I encountered the same scene: a strong bully, with unlimited power. It amazed me that the ones he squeezed and humiliated took it, even though they were many and he was one. They looked upon their master with trepidation and even delight.

I knew that when I came face to face with Roman. He and his brother were nicknamed the Romanov dynasty, because of the similarity of the name with the house of Romanovs, who ruled Russia for three hundred years.

I had nowhere to retreat. Having beaten Rickets, I called down upon myself the wrath of the mighty Roman. Reprisal awaited me back at the dormitory.

Holding my breath, I opened the door and crossed the threshold. A metal mug flew across the room and dug into the door, near my ear. I didn't know if Roman had missed by accident or purposely thrown wide just to scare me, paralyze my will. I froze on the spot. Roman reclined on his cot like a fat bullfrog and smiled at me, his upper lip curled in a predatory way, revealing small, gapped teeth.

"What are you standing there for?" he asked without raising his voice. "Come in. We'll talk."

"Let's talk," I tried to say, but my lips didn't quite obey me.

"Hey, punk! My pants!" Roman waved his stubby arm. "Fast!"

Several boys rushed to his black cotton pants, neatly hung on the back of the only chair in the room. One beat the rest, grabbed the pants out from under their noses, and handed them to Roman with a cringing smile. It was Tiny, Syoma Silberman.

Blood rushed to my head. The base ingratitude and the slavish tiny soul of the person I had defended so stunned me that I came to my senses. My fear disappeared, and I got fighting mad. I was ready for any outcome. There was no point in counting on any sympathy, much less help, from the others. I had to rely on myself. I knew from previous fights to be calm and act with calculation. I worried only when there was uncertainty. But now things were all too clear. I was alone against an experienced and treacherous foe, who would not be above any dirty trick. On his side was the full support of the entire horde of pathetic slaves, already whispering in anticipation of the fascinating spectacle of the punishment of an idiot who dared raise his tail against the master. They didn't want victory for me, their defender, but for their oppressor Roman.

Roman put on his pants, disdainfully pushing away his eager serfs. He didn't bother with his shirt. He remained in his coarse white undershirt. The snarling smile never left his face, and his eyes were narrowed, with psychopathic hatred boiling in them.

It was a scary sight, and if the pause had stretched out any more, I would have lost my self-possession. Bullies like Roman had routines for terrifying their victims into a state of rabbitlike terror. This was achieved through the indolent slowness, an unflagging smile—a sign of complete calm and confidence—and the special sibilant pronunciation of words that made you flush and chill alternately.

Luckily, the moment of truth came before I was broken psychologically. Roman picked up a pool cue.

"If we're going to fight, we should be on equal terms," I said, hoping my voice didn't betray my anxiety. "You're not a punk like them, Roman. Or don't you trust your fists?"

Slowly, reluctantly, he put the cue down on his cot, and I saw his bulldog face turn pale. He realized that I wasn't afraid of him. He had lost his advantage—a hypnotic fear that overwhelmed his opponents.

The audience was stunned too. They had just been moving the table from the middle of the room, to create an arena for the fight, and now they were frozen on their cots, staring in disbelief at their idol, who was losing his aura right before their eyes, and at me, who was already eliciting their respect and fear. I didn't flinch before Roman himself! The idol crashed from his pedestal, confusing the slaves.

Roman chickened out.

"We'll talk another time," he spat through clenched teeth and went to the door, walking around me as I stood in the middle of the room. Looking around in fear, Rickets rushed out after him.

When the door slammed behind them, silence reigned for a long, long time in the room, and no one budged. Everyone seemed to be listening, to see if Roman had changed his mind and was coming back. Then they began shouting.

"The hell with Roman!"

"The end!"

"Hey, guys! No more Roman!"

"I spit in his eyes!"

All around me I saw boys leaping on the cots in a frenzied dance. I heard the wild delight of recent slaves who have lost their fears. They looked upon me with amazement and adoration. With every moment I grew more entrenched in the role of new idol.

"Enough!" I waved my arm, and the cries died down. Smiles slid from their faces, making way for anticipation and attention. Now my word was becoming their command.

"This is the end of the Romanov dynasty!" I proclaimed. I felt like a revolutionary, like my favorite historical hero, Garibaldi, who announced the end of tyranny to his people and the advent of long-awaited freedom. "Now you are free! Everyone on his own! Don't give your food rations to anyone! Don't serve anyone and don't let anyone pick on you! Understand?"

"We understand!" my people cried out from the cots, but I could see from their bewildered faces that it was far from clear.

"There are no punks and no bosses! Everyone's

equal!" I continued and even threw in a little humor. "No one licks anyone's ass! You can only lick your own . . . if your tongue will reach it."

My people got the joke and roared with laughter.

"What happens when Roman comes back?" someone asked uncertainly.

"He'll be as quiet as water and as low as grass," I promised.

I headed for the door to give them a chance to realize what had happened by themselves. But as soon as I took the first step, Tiny Silberman rushed over and blocked the door with his puny body, holding his hands beseechingly at his chest.

"Don't go! They're waiting in ambush! They'll stick a knife between your ears!"

And he looked at me with those sad Jewish eyes, shining with loyalty and love. He was undoubtedly right. Roman and Rickets were quite capable of waiting for me around the nearest corner with knives in their pockets.

"Don't go! Don't!" They shouted from their cots, as if they were afraid to be left without me. "They'll slice you up! That's for sure!"

The thought gave me the creeps. But I certainly couldn't appear fainthearted now. I didn't have the right to besmirch my hero's toga. I said nothing and went out the door.

Roman and Ivan did not return to the room. At least, none of us saw them, even though we didn't close our eyes until very late. I was the last to fall asleep, worried that I would be stabbed in bed.

I woke up alive and unharmed. All my clothes as

well as my shoes and my coat and cap had disappeared. Roman's and Ivan's things were gone too. The brothers had run away, robbing me and taking their own stuff. It was a petty, pathetic revenge, which totally discredited the former master in the eyes of his recent subjects.

I sat in my underwear on my cot, while the room got ready for work. I sat as Roman had, but with a difference—I had nothing to wear. The guys offered me their own clothes, they respectfully added a pillow behind my back, and they brought me not only my portion from the cafeteria, but a mound of extra pieces of bread, which they cut from their rations.

I refused everything, confusing them completely. They couldn't understand. Having overturned their master, I automatically became the new master. And they were prepared to serve without question. The logic of life as they saw it was being disrupted—the laws of the jungle which they accepted blindly were not being followed. Unbelieving, I saw that they found their freedom a burden, that they felt lonely without a master's hard eye on them. They needed a new ruler, and I was it for them. But I was a strange and incomprehensible one, who wouldn't take any power.

At noon I was given a new outfit from the warehouse, and when we all returned from the shop, I dressed and we all went in to dinner together. Once again that mound of extra bread appeared before my bowl, and I looked at the bluish, skinny faces of my "subjects" and ordered them to take back the pieces of bread and eat them in front of me. They couldn't believe their ears. I repeated it. Then one meek hand reached toward the bread, and another trembling hand followed.

Back in the dorm everyone crawled to his cot. Despair hung in the air.

"Boys," I said, "be men. There's no more dictator. We now have a republic. Freedom for everyone. Do you understand what that means? Answer me!"

There was silence from the cots. I cursed and went out, slamming the door. But I didn't leave—I stayed outside and listened. There was an uproar in the room. They were deriding me in chorus, mocking me for being a fool.

I flung open the door. But the noise didn't abate. They didn't pay any attention to me. I had ceased to exist as far as they were concerned. If anyone's eyes did meet mine, they held nothing but contempt and challenge.

Tiny Silberman went behind my back, and from the peals of laughter that ensued, I guessed he was holding two fingers behind my head. I felt such weariness that it seemed like too much trouble to turn around and punch him.

I wanted to cry, but that would be the end of me. Just as stray dogs with their tails between their legs are capable of chasing anyone who runs from them tearing him to bits, this horde of slaves could attack me.

I went to my cot and began packing my things in a sack. Gradually silence spread over the room. I packed the new uniform I was given at noon, I stuck my blanket and work shoes in the sack, put on my coat and, without a word, left the room.

I don't know what went on after I left. Perhaps they

began fearfully testing one another, to see who would assume the mantle of power and become the boss. They could not imagine life without a boss.

I walked along the snow in early twilight to the nearby railroad line. There was a sharp turn in the tracks just there, and the trains slowed down, so you could hop a freight train without risk. I was on the run. Alone again. Tears fell in my soul. I wept for my faith in freedom, which in my innocence I thought people desperately needed.

7

The iron floor of the railroad car lurched beneath me at steady intervals, whenever the wheels hit the joints in the track.

It was a freight car, for transporting coal. It had a metal bottom and high wooden walls—no roof, because the coal was loaded from above. Now the car was empty. Tiny crumbs of coal rolled around on the metal floor. The unloaded cars were called empties. Long trains of empties traveled to pick up coal, from the Urals to Siberia through an enormous plain, as big as all of Europe, called the Western Siberian Depression.

I was the only passenger, a stowaway. A kid in a padded jacket and canvas shoes with rubber soles. A civilian cap, not part of my uniform, was pulled over my head, down to my eyebrows. This was the second day of my travels, and the ashes that settled in blue-gray flakes from the smoke billowing overhead had sprinkled my clothes and face.

In the whole train that extended half a mile among the groves of birches and endless green steppe on both sides of the double-track road, there were only two other people—the engineer and the fireman. I hadn't seen them. There were at least twenty cars between mine and the engine. They didn't know that I existed. It was hundreds of miles between stations, and we didn't stop at every one. When we did, it was only to fill up on water or change crews. I slept in the corner of the car, rolled up in the coal dust, my arms around my knees. It was my second day without a crumb of food or a drop of water.

You could buy food only with ration cards, and I didn't have any. You could also get food at the station markets without cards, paying black-market prices for a couple of boiled potatoes and a mug of milk. I had money—it was stuck with sweat in my shoes. But I slept through the stops, awakening only from the rumble and knocking of the bumpers between cars when the train took off with a jerk.

I was on the run. Again. My train of empties headed through endless, grain-filled Siberia, far away from the old places, where hunger almost did me in.

The herds of boys riding the rails in the Urals often talked about bountiful Siberia, but very few dared to set off on such a long journey into the unknown.

At the end of my car was a wooden seat by the brake lever. I climbed up on an iron metal ladder, sat in the seat, held on to the metal lever with both hands, and let the wind, mixed with smoke, hit my face and chest. All the cars, gaping empty, were in view now. So was the engine's tender, where I could sometimes make out the barely visible black shape of the fireman shoveling coal.

Rich Siberia passed on both sides. Herds of spotted cows grazed in meadows, and a shepherd boy in his father's jacket stood still, watching our train rattle by. A truck raised dust on the horizon, or a curly herd of sheep passed. Then the birches and the green fields.

But most often there were no people at all. Siberia was not densely populated. Without people, my only pleasure was in oncoming trains, roaring toward us and whizzing by on the track next to us. They were freight trains like ours, but with two steam engines pulling, carrying coal to the Urals. Those cars were loaded to the brim, black hills rising above the sides.

A low string of open platform cars carrying green tanks and guns rattled past. Even though it was far from the front, the tanks and cannon were camouflaged with birch and aspen branches, the leaves still green. Soldiers sat on the platforms, digging their spoons into aluminum bowls and grinning at me.

The coal pieces crumbled under my weight, turning to dust. I was dizzy with hunger and thirst, and with dry, cracked lips I whispered a vow not to sleep and miss another station; I would run down to the market and get something to eat.

The hungry rumbling of my stomach had been with me a long time, since the first winter of the war. But still, something had always ended up in my belly. At school there was the legal ration of bread, damp and sticky, with gruel, and a grain or two of barley. Perhaps a drop of meat fat floating in the murky water like a gold blob that I fished out with the tip of my tongue.

And so, thinking about food, I paced back and forth in the car, occasionally deafened by the thunder of another train and constantly sprinkled by ashes settling from the twisted cloud of the engine's smoke. Finally, exhausted, no longer thinking straight, I sat down in the corner, on the sun-warmed metal floor, and sank into oblivion.

I was awakened by a sharp jolt and the screech of metal. The car was slowly gathering speed. That meant I had missed another stop and another hungry night lay ahead of me. I tried to spit in disgust, but nothing fell from my lips. My mouth was dry and rough, so rough that it hurt to swallow.

The train was picking up speed, and the *clickety-clack* grew faster, mocking me: "Slept again, slept again, stupid, stupid. Starve to death."

I looked at the darkening sky, where the smoke curled, and beyond the smoke the first stars glimmered. Inside the car the darkness gathered, until it was suddenly replaced by a flash of light. We had passed under a lamppost, and it lit the car from above, forming shifting shadows. Then we were swallowed by the dark. And then a lamppost chased it away. The train was passing a large station.

Squinting in the bright light, I managed to see a human figure, appearing and disappearing in the changing light at the end of my car. Someone had climbed into my car. I waited for the next light and discovered that it was a girl, about my age. The girl was blond, with two short braids sticking out from the sides of her head. Instead of ribbons, she had tied them with pieces of bandage. Her mother must work in a hospital, I thought. She wore a sweater that hung down to her knees. So I couldn't tell if she was wearing a skirt or if the sweater was all she had on. Her bare legs stuck out.

I didn't see much of her face. I didn't want to. She had a pug nose, I saw that.

She stood without moving, and I guessed that she had seen me. I also guessed that she was afraid.

I really must have looked scary. I was huddled up, a typical hobo riding the rails, cap low over my eyes, unwashed face covered with soot. I didn't move but silently, even maliciously, kept my eyes on her, the way a cat looks at a mouse trapped in a corner.

Tired of standing, the girl sat down in the corner on the diagonal from me. She sat down on the metal floor, with an almost bare bottom. The edge of the sweater wouldn't protect her from the burning cold of the metal. I had spent two nights in that car. I was wearing two pairs of trousers and long underwear, but by midnight my butt grew icy, and I had to jump and run around to warm up.

I wrapped my warm quilted jacket around me and waited with a crooked grin to see what would happen. The cold wouldn't let her sit long. I was sure of that.

The wheels clicked under my butt and under hers

too. The car swayed—we did too. The stars emitted a cold, inanimate light.

My calculations proved correct. The girl was getting chilled. She was squirming in her place, getting up on all fours, never taking her eyes off me, as if magnetized.

I didn't move. I waited to see what would be next. I was still amusing myself. The girl had a choice. Freeze solid in her corner at a safe distance from me, or overcome her fear, and beg for warmth from me, the monster.

I almost thought I could hear her pathetic whimpering. A cold puppy whimpers like that in front of a locked door.

She couldn't take it. On her hands and knees, she crawled from her corner in my direction. And I thought how the coal must be scratching her knees, though she must not have felt the pain for the cold and fear.

The distance between us diminished. I stayed in my place, and she crawled like a dog. She went one yard—then another. Then she stopped, her lips trembling, her teeth chattering. And something between a moan and a howl reached my tense ears.

"Bluh-bluh-bluh . . ."

It contained a plea: "Take pity . . . don't let me die. . . . Save me. . . ."

She was so close now that I could see the gauze bandages on her braids; her eyes, round like a bird's; her trembling pointy chin; and her thin pathetic neck in the scoop of her sweater.

"Bluh . . . bluh . . . bluh . . ."

Her shoulders shook, either with cold or with sobs—probably both.

She forgot her fears. She wanted only one thing: a little warmth. I could give her that warmth, I could save her, comfort her. I could protect her.

Suddenly I felt a chill. My skin no longer felt my own. Everything that I did afterward I did unconsciously, not understanding why I was doing it. My crude disdain for the girl disappeared. My lonely embittered wolf-cub heart was scalded.

With unresponding fingers I unbuttoned my padded jacket and flung it open. The girl was stunned. Like a rabbit on its hind legs, she rose up on her knees and, still unbelieving, looked at me. Then she rushed to me, threw herself at my side as if I were a hot oven. She huddled up close, tucking her legs in and resting her knees on my hip.

I closed the coat, covering her head. I carefully tucked in the separating halves.

All of her fit under my coat. She buried her face under my arm, and I felt her fast, hot breath. Her shoulders were still heaving, her whole body was trembling. And she still hadn't stopped her soft whimper.

"Bluh, bluh, bluh . . ."

It wasn't a howl anymore, but a sweet sleepy mumble replaced by the deep breathing of sleep.

The chill was over. Her body relaxed. Her arms, which had been around me, slipped away.

My chin rested on the top of her head and I inhaled the scent of her hair.

I felt hot. I was panting, as if after a long run, and

I tried to control my breath, so her sleep wouldn't be disturbed. I was engulfed in a wave of sweet tenderness. I felt incredibly strong, capable of defending and protecting a weak creature in need of my aid. My legs fell asleep and the pins and needles were bothering me, but I didn't even think of moving. I protected her sleep, and I was filled with new emotions. My eyes stung.

At that moment, under the cold twinkle of the stars, under the blue scrolls of smoke to the steady rhythm of the train, the man in me awoke—strong, kind, and tender. I had never felt better in my life.

I fell into a deep, peaceful sleep.

I awoke from a jolt that clanged the bumper disks. The train was leaving a station. I had missed another one.

It was dawn, and there wasn't a single star in the sky. In the far end of the car the gate, slightly ajar, showed light. That light spelled worry for me.

I moved my hand over my chest. There was no one under my coat. My eyes quickly examined the whole car and once again rested on the open gate.

The girl wasn't in the car. She had gotten out at the station through that crack. She left while I slept, without waking me, without saying anything in farewell.

The train was picking up speed. Swaying, I went down the car to the opening and looked out. Empty wet meadows sped away. The station where the girl had gotten off was out of sight by now. I felt a chill.

I couldn't understand what was happening to me. Before that night I had never been bored by myself, and I had never felt lonely. And now I felt terribly uncomfortable, and the car, which I paced back and forth in, was like a cage, a prison.

I could no longer be alone.

I had grown up.

How long I was unconscious, I don't know. When somebody shook me, and I managed to pry open my gummy lids, I discovered that I was lying on the metal floor of an empty freight car. The sky was blue high above me, and very close to me was a strange, mustached, wrinkled face with a homemade cigarette butt stuck in its lower lip.

"He's alive," a man said. "Well, buddy, thank the Lord that I looked into this car, or we would have loaded the coal on top of you. Get out, now that you're awake. I'll help you."

He pulled me out like a sack and wanted to sit me down on the black, oil-stained ground near the tracks, but I couldn't sit up and fell on my back.

"Well, have a lie down," the voice said. "I'll fetch

the doc. . . . We'll bring a stretcher. . . . You lie there, kid."

On either side of me red coal cars stretched in an endless line. Above them towered black trestles, and conveyor belts dropped coal into the cars, the biggest lumps making a loud thump as they landed. When the cars were filled to the top, they pulled away, bumpers creaking, hauled by the engines I couldn't see.

I was deep in Siberia. In the Kuzbass, the Kuznetsk Coal Basin. When I turned over on my belly and crawled under the freight car over the rails, I saw the green steppe—and on its level surface, like dirty, suppurating boils, the dark smoking cones of the mine dumps. Mountains of unproductive ores were piled up, removed from the mines as they dug through to the rich coal-bearing veins.

The air smelled of coal and coke, and that special odor that comes from the oil-soaked soil around railroad tracks.

I crawled downhill through the gravel until my face hit grass. I did not want them to come for me with a stretcher, I didn't want to be moved or touched. I was dying, and I wanted to die in peace.

My head was burning—my fever must have been around 104° F. My stomach burned too as if I had eaten ground glass. To still the pain a bit, I rolled over and up, knees up to my stomach, and arms pressed to my chest.

I could hear voices. The man with the mustache must have brought orderlies.

I didn't respond to their calls. Then the voices were

buried in the rumble and screech of the freight cars. I passed out again, and when I awoke, the sun was high in the sky. It was afternoon.

I don't know why, but suddenly I didn't want to die anymore. Something urged me to crawl farther into the steppe, along the grass that smelled so sharp and fresh. I crawled on my belly, propelling myself with my elbows and pulling my knees along. I didn't have the strength to get up on all fours.

The farther I got from the tracks, the thicker and higher rose the grass. Buttercups twinkled, and there were tiny, multipetaled white flowers. My lips found the fuzzy, juicy leaf of a clover plant, and I bit it off. The sour freshness dripped into my dry mouth. I sought other cloverleaves in the grass.

I crawled without a path, right into the unmowed steppe. Crickets leaped out of the grass before my face, hiding until I got closer, and then hopping up with a dry crackle once again.

The movement and the sun made me hot. Acrid sweat poured into my eyes and down my cheeks. The first thing to be left behind in the grass was my seven-pointed blue cheviot cap.

Then, like a snake shedding its old skin, I crawled out of my padded quilted coat.

The sun had slipped all the way to the edge of the sky when I sank into an exhausted sleep, my last slow thoughts convincing me that this time I really was dying and would never awake.

I heard a dog barking and children's voices. I opened my eyes and shut them again. A black dog face hung above me, and a red tongue roughly licked my cheek and nose.

"He's alive, alive," the children I couldn't see chanted. "Mama, come here. . . . He's alive."

The dog's muzzle disappeared with a whimper—he must have been pushed away—and now the sky was blocked by a woman's head in a dark scarf. Her flat, coarse face could have been hewn out of dry wood. It looked like a monkey's face with its flat nose and broad nostrils and long upper lip above a narrow slit of a mouth. The eyes were small and sharp, with slanting upper lids.

"Baba Yaga, the witch," I thought.

"What's this you're up to?" Baba Yaga asked sternly.

"I'm dying," I said, my parched lips cracking.

"Couldn't you find a better place? You had to do it on my doorstep?"

"Sorry," I whispered.

"Sorry, sorry," she mocked, still squinting at me. "Get up. You'll wear out your sides."

I shook my head to let her know that I didn't have the strength to get up.

"Oh, so you're stubborn," she drawled. "Lordy! Look at you! You're all black!"

I smiled, and her upper lip moved just like the monkey's at the zoo.

"Well, girls," she ordered. "Drag that slugabed to the house. Lift him by the arms and feet. We'll wash you up, dress you in clean clothes, lay you down under the icons, and then you can die like a decent person."

And here I got a look at the girls. Five of them about

my age or younger. One was a hunchback and looked like a midget in the circus.

But I learned all that later, when I recovered in the house of Polina Sergeyevna. That was the name of the woman, the mother of five girls. All there was of the house was a mounded roof, overgrown with grass.

Polina Sergeyevna lived in a dugout, and the walls were earth smeared with clay and lime. The floor was dirt too, tramped down hard, like rock. Only the ceiling was made of wood, supported by three logs digging into the ground. There was only one window, as small as in a freight car. To reach the door, you had to go down five steps dug out of the earth. The girls dragged me down those steps, chattering and shoving, into the only room, half of which was occupied by a broad plank bed covered with a colorful patchwork quilt. The whole family slept on that bed, all six of them. And before the mister—that's how Polina Sergeyevna referred to her husband—was called up, all seven slept there. The husband went off to war and didn't even have time to send them a letter. He was killed.

The rest of the house was taken up by a whitewashed and smoke-stained stove and a clean-scraped uncovered table with two wooden benches.

They bathed me in a dented tin tub that they used for boiling the laundry. They pushed the table over to the wall and put the tub on the dirt floor, warming water in a cast-iron pot. While it heated, I sat on a bench with my back against the wall and tried to keep from falling off.

The girls bustled noisily around their mother, ex-

125

cited by the presence of a stranger who might just drop dead at any moment. They hauled water from the well, added firewood to the stove, eager to be first to help their mother. When the tub was filled with hot water, Polina Sergeyevna shouted at them and sent them out, leaving her hunchbacked elder daughter, Raya, as her helper.

"Well, little man, take off your underpants. We'll wash off the crust," she said to me.

I couldn't manage by myself; my fingers disobeyed. I couldn't even do the buttons.

"Let me," said Raya, looking at me with compassion in her round watery eyes beneath thick white lashes. Her too-large head was supported by a short neck, and her light hair was combed smoothly with a center part and two tight pigtails stuck out in front of her ears. She had a nasal voice and the intelligence of a small child. Later Polina Sergeyevna told me that Raya had stopped developing at the age of six, when her drunken father had dropped her headfirst on the ground.

The father, apparently, was quite a drinker. He left another trace of his alcoholism in the house besides Raya's hump. Two other daughters, aged ten and six, had the same name: Katya, short for Katerina. When the fifth daughter was born, the father lost all hope of having a son and got so drunk that when he went to register the birth, he forgot that he already had a daughter named Katya, and named this one Katerina too. They called the sisters Big Katya and Little Katya.

When I later asked Polina Sergeyevna about her deceased husband, she sighed without judgment: "He drank, of course . . . but who doesn't?"

Hunchbacked Raya got on her knees in front of me and unlaced my shoes. Polina Sergeyevna pulled my shirt over my head, and I melted in her hands.

They took off everything, even my underwear. Polina Sergeyevna told Raya to take my filthy, stiff clothes from the house and leave them far off in the grass.

"And take the shoes," she called after her. "They must be full of lice too."

At the very bottom of my shoes lay a sticky pile of money that I had gotten for the sale of my uniform, but I was too tired to tell Raya to be careful.

"Don't you have a hat?" Polina Sergeyevna asked.

I remembered my seven-cornered cap and told her as clearly as I could that I had lost it and my brand-new coat while I was crawling. She sent the girls out into the steppe and they found my cap and coat.

I sat chest deep in the hot water, holding on to the tub's tin sides. Raya propped me up from the back with her wet hands to keep me from falling. Polina Sergeyevna, sleeves rolled up, scrubbed my bony body ruthlessly with a stiff brush, and to make up for the soap she didn't have, she rubbed ashes from the stove into my skin. The water turned black from my dirt and the ashes, and Raya poured clean water from a pitcher onto my head.

I flopped around like a sunflower in the wind in Polina Sergeyevna's enormous iron hands, both when she washed me and when she dried me, wrapping me in a large sheet full of holes and carrying me like a child to the bed.

127

And that was the first time I heard the loving words from her lips:

"Nestling! You're my little nestling."

That warm word was imbued with so much tenderness, and Polina Sergeyevna said it with such suppressed love, that I could tell how much she wanted a son.

I fell asleep as soon as her hands tucked me in under the quilt. I slept the whole day and the whole night and didn't hear or feel the girls get into the bed. Both Katyas, Big and Little; hunchbacked Raya; and two others, Tonya and Zina. They lay down in a row by the wall. And their mother lay on her side on the edge, afraid to bother me and worried that I might fall off. I had a fever, I was delirious. Later Raya, pouting like a baby, showed me the bruises on her shoulder and side from my flailing elbows.

Polina Sergeyevna felt my hot damp forehead with her dry rough hand, and when I muttered quite grown-up curses, she hugged me and whispered right in my ear, as if playing, blowing in it:

"Shhshh, silly. It's not nice to say words like that. Sleep, nestling, sleep."

At dawn I opened my eyes. The fever had dropped, but my whole body ached, as if I had been beaten. And I was so weak that I didn't want to stir or talk, but just drink—drink endlessly, without lifting my head, just swallowing. My dry lips held tight to the rough edge of the metal mug that Polina Sergeyevna held by my face. The milk she gave me was straight from the cow. She had poured it through a sieve into the clay pitcher. I drank, gulping, grunting, unable to stop. As soon as

I emptied the mug, I waited eagerly for her to fill it again.

"Look at you!" Polina Sergeyevna pretended to be upset. "How can you fit so much in? What a pig! You'll pee in the bed. Then you'll be so ashamed before the girls."

The girls were sleeping next to me, smacking their lips sweetly.

"You sleep too," she said, and tucked me in. "If you get thirsty, wake up Raya. She'll bring you some milk. Milk is the best medicine. It'll get rid of your illness, like it never happened. And then we'll have a healthy man in our house, a breadwinner and protector."

She grinned crookedly and winked at me.

"Sleep now . . . nestling."

An icon, old and chipped, hung in the corner, and on it I could make out the gilt face of Saint Nicholas. An elongated narrow face, straight hair, and very sad eyes, as if he couldn't bear looking at the lack of space Polina Sergeyevna's family lived in. The votive light before the icon was not lit; they were saving kerosene.

Polina Sergeyevna worked from dawn to dusk at the farm. She milked and fed a dozen cows, and she cleaned out their manure. She did all the work with her bare hands, and that's why they were as big and clumsy as rakes.

The children were left at home alone, and now they had me as well, sick and helpless. As she left, Polina Sergeyevna stopped in front of the icon, gave Saint Nicholas a quick appraising glance, and said trustingly, "Keep an eye on them, Nicholas. You're the only man with a brain in the house. Don't let them play with fire . . . or fight . . . or hurt that sick one. . . . Understand? When I get back . . . things better be fine."

And she left, closing the door.

Saint Nicholas was something of a house spirit for Polina Sergeyevna. He was someone she could talk to like an adult. She couldn't really talk with little kids. And Raya didn't count—she was retarded.

After she cleaned up the supper dishes and washed the stove, Polina would sit down on the bench with a pile of clothes, pull the kerosene lamp closer, squint to thread the needle, and get on with her mending. Sighing and muttering to herself, she gave the icon a questioning and suspicious look. She was just talking, so he would know how things were on earth.

I never did decide whether Polina Sergeyevna believed in God or not. There was no church in the state farm village. It had not been closed or destroyed, as in other villages. The village had been built in Soviet times. The Soviets made the farms comfortable for the cows, but the people lived in cavelike dugouts, without water and with kerosene light.

Polina Sergeyevna's children were not baptized. In school they were taught that God did not exist. Their mother didn't say anything about it. It was not wise to dispute with the authorities. But she kept the icon. As soon as her husband was called up, she hung it in the corner where an icon should be. Next to it she hung a picture of Stalin in his military uniform, thinking that this way she satisfied everyone and hurt no one.

"Now, listen," she said, looking up at Saint Nicholas and then back to her sewing. She told him about the problems of the farm, the foreman who was no help at all and was the only man on the farm. She confided her household cares. And then, as if realizing, she shrugged and chuckled:

"What am I telling you for? Pointless."

But after a few moments of silence she would sigh and mutter once again, "Oh, Nick, Nick . . . Nicholas. What are you staring at? Think I'm a stupid woman? . . . Don't know what I'm talking about? You're laughing at me, Nick. . . . Don't. Things are bad for me, Nicholas . . . so bad."

I grew still, holding my breath. I knew that Polina Sergeyevna was speaking her most private thoughts.

She complained about her widowhood, her life ruined by a drunkard husband and heavy work. She complained that she had aged before her time. And God only knew if she had enough strength to bring her girls out into the world and set them on their feet.

Sleep overtook her, and her plaints turned into indistinguishable muttering. She must have pricked her finger on the needle; she swore crudely, like a man, and then pushed the rags from her lap. She stretched until her bones creaked, straightening her shoulders and moving her gnarled fingers that looked like crab claws. Her mouth stretched wide in a long yawn. She got up from the bench and looked slyly over her shoulder at her nocturnal confidant:

"What am I telling you for? What do you men understand of our affairs?"

Her enormous shadow moved along the wall and

131

covered almost the entire plank ceiling. She was approaching the wall. Beyond the portrait of Stalin hung a clock with a dented metal face painted with a picture of women in red kerchiefs holding yellow sheaves. Two chains hung down from the clock. One was short and ended in a ring, the other hung down to the floor. Tied to it was an iron padlock, used in place of the regular weight. She took hold of the ring and pulled the chain so that the padlock crept up to the clock's face. Then she took the pins from her hair, holding them in her mouth. When she came back to the table, she sighed and then put out the lamp's flame with her bare fingers, vanishing into the dark. I could hear the rustle of her clothing as it came off. Then her breath tickled my ear in a warm wave as she whispered:

"Shhhhh. . . . Move over, nestling. . . . Let me lay down my bones."

I didn't get up for several days. When Polina Sergeyevna was out, Raya took her place. The humpbacked girl shouted at the others with her stuffed-nose voice, bustled like an adult around the stove, and fed me with a spoon, sitting on the edge of the bed and digging her sharp elbow into my side. The other girls teased her but did everything she demanded, especially if it concerned me.

I became the center of the whole family's life: the only man in the house, the boy they had always wanted.

They were poor, like all working-class people, getting meager sustenance on their ration cards. They added potatoes from their garden and some milk from the cow. They sold most of the milk to buy something to cover the girls' bodies.

Now I was drinking up all the milk, and eating the potatoes and part of their bread ration. I didn't have ration cards and I wasn't entitled to any food.

While I recovered in bed, I tried to figure out a way to repay them.

Raya amused me with conversation.

"How old are you?" she asked.

"Fourteen . . . soon."

"Baby," she said, wrinkling up her little nose. "I'm older than you. Sixteen."

Raya didn't reach my shoulder.

"A bride," I said.

"Sez you," she said, flinging her blond pigtail at me. "No one would take me. I have a hump."

"I'll marry you," I said with a wink.

"Sez you," she laughed. "You'll leave and not even remember me."

I wasn't embarrassed by Raya. That's why she could sleep next to me. Raya on my left, and Polina Sergeyevna on my right. The other girls were closer to the wall, whispering and squealing, excited to have a boy under the same blanket.

Once Polina Sergeyevna brought home a piece of meat wrapped in a rag. There had been no meat at home, and the girls had forgotten its smell. They had slaughtered a piglet at the farm, and swallowing her pride, Polina Sergeyevna asked for a piece of meat— for her boy. They knew all about me at the farm. They used to ask: How's your starveling? And so for me, the starveling, she got a piece of pork, a pink strip of meat with a white layer of fat.

The girls were tense. They stared at the stove, never taking their eyes from the pieces of meat jumping in the skillet. The smell from the stove was enough to make us all dizzy.

I was seated at the table for the occasion. I sat in my trousers, but without my shirt. Just my undershirt, freshly washed. There was an empty plate on the table, a knife and fork, and a piece of bread. I felt as if I were preparing for a solemn ritual.

Polina Sergeyevna did not save a single piece of that delicious-smelling meat for herself or the girls. She scraped everything onto my plate.

"Eat, nestling," she said, and sat down opposite me. The girls sat on the bench and looked away from the steaming plate.

"What about them?" I asked.

"They'll manage," Polina Sergeyevna said.

"What about you?"

"What about me? You think I've never seen meat before?"

I chewed without looking up. And even though the wonderful smell intoxicated me, I had difficulty swallowing.

"What are you staring at?" Polina Sergeyevna called. "You're ruining his appetite. Go wipe the skillet with some bread. Save your mother the trouble of washing it."

The girls jumped up from the table noisily, grabbed the pieces of bread Raya cut, and huddled around the stove, pushing and shoving to get at the pan.

"Don't eat the skillet," their mother teased, and looked at me with an apologetic smile. "Young and old—they're all as silly as can be. . . . Eat, eat, nestling, while it's hot."

I repaid their kindness even before I got out of bed—in a bad way. I had picked up the mange, a vile disease, in the freight trains, and now I infected them all. Polina Sergeyevna didn't catch it, but the girls, one after another, began scratching violently and soon were covered with pus-filled sores from head to toe.

Polina Sergeyevna sighed and grumbled, but didn't scold me. She went to the paramedic and brought back a large jar of black salve that smelled like tar. She smeared all of us, one at a time, turning us into spotty black urchins. She was particularly careful in smearing me. I sat naked on the bench and she smeared the salve onto my goose-bumpy skin.

"Don't be shy, fellow. What are you covering your private parts for? Think I've never seen any? Look at that, Lord! Come on, spread those legs! Look where the disease has crept! Right to the very spot."

She scooped it all up in her hand, making me blush, and began rubbing in the salve.

"Look at him. . . . What are you . . . circumcised?"

I nodded.

"What do you think of that!" Polina Sergeyevna gasped playfully. "Who am I sheltering in my house? A Tatar, maybe?"

"No . . . I'm a Jew."

Polina Sergeyevna's finger froze over my salved hips.

"What sort of people is that?"

"Ordinary." I shrugged.

"Our Soviet kind?"

"What else?" I was almost insulted.

"Hitler is killing them . . . those Jew," Big Katya piped up from the bed.

"What do *you* know," Polina Sergeyevna chided.

"I saw it in the paper," Katya said in an injured tone.

"Well, then, there's nothing to discuss," her mother said and went back to rubbing in the salve.

When she was done she helped me with my underpants and shirt, which immediately stuck to my body. I got in under the blanket with the girls. Polina Sergeyevna washed off the black gunk from her hand and said, as if summing up:

"There, girls, see how many people there are in the world. . . . And all just as good as us Russians."

Then she squinted over at Saint Nicholas, who looked down sadly from his corner.

"That's the way it is, Nick. . . ."

9

I was full. I was lying on wheat, digging into it with my feet. The bready smell of the grain tickled my nostrils. Even if I forced myself, I couldn't eat—no room. How wonderful, how sweet, not to be hungry.

"Hey, little man," I heard a voice, a female voice next to my wagon. I lifted my crumpled face, pocked with grain imprints, and looked up.

A woman's head in a white kerchief knotted at the neck showed above the edge of the wagon. A young woman was smiling shyly, stretching her dry, chapped lips and revealing even white teeth and pink gums.

I raised myself up on my elbow and tugged the reins. The horses stopped obediently. I could see her from top to bottom: sturdy bare feet with dark cracks along the ankle; a reddish shirt made of rough homespun fabric clung to her hips; a light, dust-covered shirt with dark circles of dampness under the arms was tucked into the skirt.

She was looking me over too.

"Hey, little man," she drawled meekly, the way people beg for alms. "Give me some grain."

And she took out a folded sack from under her arm and shook it and smoothed it out.

"My children are hungry," she added. "Give me some grain for bread. . . . You have so much. No one will ever know."

"And what will you give me?" I asked, trying to sound tough and manly, but my voice sounded fragile and weak.

Her eyelashes quivered and surprise and fear flashed in her eyes.

"What could I give you?" she said with a little laugh, even more embarrassed. "I'm wearing all I own."

"Take off your skirt."

I said it casually, and her whitish brows shot up.

"What's the matter with you, fellow?"

"Nothing," I said. "If you want bread, give me your skirt."

"Is that it?" Her face cleared. "I thought . . ."

She turned her back to me, I saw her shoulder blades working as she unhooked the waistband and pushed down the skirt until it lay in a reddish puddle around her feet.

Now she was wearing a blouse and an undershirt that reached her knees. She bent over, picked up the skirt, shook off the dust, folded it neatly, first in half and then in half again, and put it on the wagon, without looking at me once.

I crawled over the grain to the back of the wagon. "Get your sack ready."

I didn't look at her, either. We were both embarrassed. I opened the hatch in the back, and the wheat poured into her sack.

"Tell me when you've got enough," I snapped.

She nodded. The wheat kept flowing and a whirlpool formed on the surface at the back, deepening quickly. I kicked grain over to fill it up.

"Enough!" she shouted. "Stop!"

I started to close the hatch.

"Enough?" I was being generous. "I can add some more."

"I don't know if I'll be able to get this home."

The sack was more than half full, fifty pounds at least.

She twisted the top of the sack and tried to lift it.

"Help me." She nodded at me.

I jumped down from the wagon. I crouched and lifted the sack from below, and she pulled it up on her back. Without saying good-bye, bent under the weight, she padded off in bare feet down the road, raising clouds of gray dust.

The bottom of her undershirt got caught under the sack, exposing her white, untanned thighs all the way up to her buttocks. She wasn't wearing anything under the shirt. My heart filled with shame, but my body aroused, I saw the mound of dark hair between her legs.

Wheels and empty wagon rattling, the horses lazily trotted me home. I was coming back at twilight from my last trip to the silo, and before bringing the horses to the stables, I turned in at our dugout. I couldn't wait to surprise Polina Sergeyevna with the skirt.

I ran down the steps, pushed the door. The meal on the stove smelled delicious. The light wasn't on yet—we were saving kerosene. The girls were sitting at the table waiting for dinner, and Polina Sergeyevna was bent over the stove, straining milk, pouring it from the pail into a clay pitcher with cheesecloth over its mouth.

"So he showed up," she grumbled, straightening. Her eyes filled with joy, even though her face remained stern. "Laborer. Smelled dinner and rushed over, eh? Where's my big spoon?"

"I've brought you something," I said with a frown, trying to hide the joy that was bursting inside me. I tossed the reddish skirt on the stool. "It's for you, Polina Sergeyevna."

"Really?" she said in surprise.

"Try it on. It's just right."

She slowly walked over to the stool, picked up the skirt, and spread it out.

"A skirt? For me? Oh, my nestling, my nestling. Our breadwinner, our strong man. Just what I needed, perfect. Mine's worn so thin, you can see right through it."

She held the skirt up and bubbled with delight.

"Oh, Mama," Raya enthused. "You're so lucky."

"There, children, look what your mother's got. New clothes. It's just like new . . . not a single hole. Where did you get it? You didn't steal it?" Polina Sergeyevna

140

squinted at me, clutching the crumpled skirt to her flat chest.

"Come on," I said in an injured tone. "I traded for it."

"Where?"

"In the steppe . . ."

"What, do skirts grow out there?" She narrowed her eyes even more sternly at me.

"Enough," I said. "Don't look a gift horse in the mouth."

"We're not used to gifts, we earn things with our hands mostly. You answer me without squirming."

"Well, I traded . . . with a woman. . . . She wanted grain . . . and traded the skirt. . . . It's just your size."

"What, was she carrying the skirt in her hands? The woman?" Polina Sergeyevna pressed.

"Why in her hands?" I laughed. "You know where skirts go."

"So what did you do? Undress her?" She even took a step away from me, still clutching the skirt.

"She took it off herself . . . and gave it to me."

"And you let her go like that, naked?"

I looked away and held my breath. I suddenly felt terrified. I clearly remembered the woman with the heavy sack on her bent back and the caught-up hem of her undershirt shamelessly exposing her.

"I don't need presents like this!"

The reddish skirt flew at my face, and I barely caught it before it hit the floor.

"Get out of here," Polina Sergeyevna said. "And don't come back until you find that woman, return the skirt, grovel at her feet, and beg for forgiveness. That's it! End of conversation."

She turned her back to me. She picked up the pail and went on straining the milk into the pitcher.

The girls were quiet at the table. They sat without stirring and stared at me with frightened eyes.

I smiled at them to cheer them up, but my smile was pathetic. Tossing the skirt in the air and whistling to cover my shame, I went out quietly.

I took out my feelings on the innocent horses. Whistling and shouting like a bandit, I whirled the ends of the reins over my head, lashing at Snokha and One-Eye, hitting their bony backs. The horses raced. The wagon rattled. I bounced on the wooden seat and had to spread my bare feet wide to keep from falling out.

I raced into the steppe, down the same road. I urged the horses constantly, not letting the tired and hungry animals slow down to a walk.

The steppe lay all around me in the night. Not a single light. Above me the sky was milky in the hazy starlight. The pale moon glowed like a slice of unripened melon. I could barely see the road. I was afraid that if we went off the road, the horses might break a leg in a gopher hole.

Finally the horses were so tired that they did not respond no matter how hard I whipped, but merely flipped their tails and went on walking. I had cooled down too. Where was I supposed to find that woman? Even if I found a village, what would I do, go from house to house, waking the dogs and knocking on windows until she answered? I fully realized the cruelty of my action, even though I tried to justify it by wanting to do something for Polina Sergeyevna, to repay her many kindnesses to me. There, you want to do good and you end up with a hell of a mess. I would carry that stain on my conscience for a long time. It would be so scary to meet Polina Sergeyevna's eyes. They wouldn't have those sparks of joy the way they did whenever she saw me. When would she ever call me her nestling again?

I hauled back and threw the reddish ball of fabric as far as I could into the dark steppe, turned the wagon around, and headed back slowly. It was after midnight when I unhitched the horses in the stable yard and led them into their stalls, giving them some hay. I tiptoed into the house, trying not to bother the sleeping girls.

Usually, no matter how late it was, the girls would be asleep in bed, and Polina Sergeyevna would be waiting up for me, darning or mending by the kerosene lamp.

She would be waiting for me, the way village women wait for the breadwinner. She would warm up dinner, and while I ate, she would sit opposite me, never taking her warm eyes from me. We would talk, and both she and I would feel peaceful and happy.

Then she would snuff the light. We would undress in the dark. I would lift the blanket and get into the warmth created by the girls, and they would mutter sleepily as they made room.

"Don't smother the girls," Polina Sergeyevna would whisper, tucking the blanket around their feet and then lying down at the edge of the bed on her side.

This time the house was dark, and no one was waiting up for me. The girls' sleepy breathing came from the bed. Polina Sergeyevna had also gone to bed, but I couldn't tell in the dark whether she was asleep or lying with her eyes open.

I felt around the stove for the remainder of the dinner, so as not to wake anyone, and then decided to go to bed.

I undressed and didn't even know what to do. I didn't dare climb under the blanket with them. I would have to get past Polina Sergeyevna, who was on the end, and that would mean unavoidable talk.

I spread my shirt and trousers on the floor and lay down naked, my fist curled under my cheek. I held my breath.

The wall clock with the lock for a weight ticked quietly.

The moon shone weakly through the window. I could see the dull glimmer of the gilt frame of the icon of Saint Nicholas. Now it seemed to me that Saint Nicholas was laughing, peering at me from his corner.

As I lay on the floor, for the first time ever under that roof, I felt myself to be a stranger, an outsider.

"Listen, fellow," Polina Sergeyevna said softly, but not in a sleepy voice. As I had thought, she wasn't asleep. "Find yourself a place to live."

I didn't stir. After a pause, she added, "The girls are growing up. . . . It's not right for them to be under the same blanket with a man."

10

The area was called Cuckoo's Tears. The whole steppe, unplowed and unmeasured, from horizon to horizon, to the distant hills showing blue in good weather.

"That's Altai over there," old man Poleshko told me. "Altai isn't Siberia anymore."

"What is it?" I asked.

"Altai," Poleshko said, and shrugged. "There the people aren't really Russian. And if you go any farther, it's pure China. Ever heard of China?"

I nodded.

Poleshko gave me a suspicious look.

"You're lying, foreman. But lying now and then is for the best. It strengthens your authority."

The old man worried about my authority, because I held an important position for someone so young. At fourteen I was in charge of the mowing brigade. Far from the village, out in the open steppe—you could gallop all over Cuckoo's Tears, left or right, and never meet anyone. A gopher might jump out from under your horse's hoofs, or a hawk might hover overhead, but no people.

There were twenty-six under my command. Siberian peasant women, vigorous, strong, and young. Poleshko and I were the only men in all of Cuckoo's Tears. The old man was the mechanic in the brigade: He'd fix the mower if anything broke, sharpen the blades when they got dull. And he did it all practically bare-handed, with only a hammer and file. He was eighty. You meet sturdy old men like that only in Siberia. Poleshko had all his teeth, his back was straight, and his hands were like iron. When there was nothing to repair, rather than hang around the kitchen, he went out into the steppe, picked up a pitchfork, and started stacking. His arms wouldn't even tremble when he tossed a seventy-pound weight onto the very top. Even though I wasn't a weakling, I never picked up more than half what he did with my pitchfork.

The women mowed the grass, swaying in the metal seats of the horse-drawn mowers. Then they raked up the dried hay with horse rakes. But the stacking—packing up the hay for the winter into ricks as big as houses—had to be done by hand. It was heavy, straining work. Before the war, only men stacked, but now they were replaced by women, mostly widows. And the ones who weren't widowed yet hadn't seen their men in almost three years.

I had a stocky Mongolian horse called Orlik at my

disposal. As she raced around the steppe, she sometimes sank into the grass up to her ears. In Siberia the summer is short but hot. The snow, once it melts in the spring, keeps the soil damp until the frosts. And the land is unplowed, virgin soil. The grass could grow to the sky.

There were so many grasses here! Wild pea twisting its gray mustaches into swirls, and "pipes," a juicy stem like bamboo, rising in sections, with huge leaves, taller than me. Lots of juicy clover climbing underfoot in oily patches. The thick tall foliage blocked the sun, and so the flowers were pale, but their scent was intoxicating. There were lots of cuckoo's tears—the tiny purple flowers that gave the region its name.

I loved looking down from my saddle at the horse-drawn mower cutting a swath through the green, creating a corridor in the solid wall. The horses shook their heads, barely visible over the tops of the grasses, and the women in the driver's seats could be seen only if I rode into the swath. The mown grass wound itself around the cogged wheels, dripping a red, bloodlike mush. Strawberries they were, ripe and as big as a child's fist, and so sweet, you could drink strawberry tea without sugar. There were tons of strawberries in the steppe. I stuffed myself with strawberries; my stomach was bloated with them. When I grew tired of bending over to pick them, I crawled in the grass and bit off the berries. My lips and cheeks would be smeared with red. At camp a treat awaited me. The cook, the wide-hipped widow Lidka Pimnyova, mashed strawberries in a soldier's mess bowl, poured foaming milk to the top, and served it to me for dessert.

Sometimes I'd forget that there was a war on somewhere, that people were on short rations, their bellies as empty as sacks. We were allotted two cows from the farm, and there was enough milk for the whole brigade. There was plenty of grain, and more than enough strawberries. What more could anyone want?

Meat—there wasn't any meat, of course. And how much physical labor can you do without meat? Siberian peasant women are big-boned and broad. They don't shirk the hardest tasks, but they need to be fed like men.

Poleshko got meat for us. Not veal, and not pork, but gopher. The meat of the fluffy gray animals that cavorted in the grass like tailless squirrels. I wouldn't eat them at first. It was like eating mice. But then, seeing the rest eat and lick their lips, I swallowed a piece. It tasted like chicken, but even sweeter. Gophers live on a diet of grass and grain. In autumn when the wheat is harvested, they get so fat they can barely move, and then it's simple to catch them.

But in the summer, when they have only grass to eat, they're quick. At the first sign of danger they dive into their holes. They escaped from me easily, but not from old man Poleshko. He knew how to catch gophers. He ordered me to follow him and bring two buckets of water. He carried a willow switch. We found the mounds of dirt that signal the tunnel entrances. A gopher dashed in, and Poleshko just laughed. He knelt, bent the switch into a noose, and placed it over the entrance, holding the ends in his hands. And he nodded to me, go ahead, pour. I poured the water, trying to get it into the hole without spilling. As soon as it sees the water, the gopher brain decides that there is a flood and it rushes outside to escape. Its head goes right into the noose. All Poleshko had to do was squeeze the ends of the switch and pull the struggling creature out. He killed the gophers mercifully, by flicking their foreheads with his fingers. Poleshko had iron fingers. I think he could even kill something bigger than a gopher with a single flick.

He tossed the carcass over his shoulder and strode on into the steppe. I followed, with one empty bucket and one full one, to the next hole. We talked as we walked, like equals.

"Why do you have a name like that, Grandpa?" I asked. "Poleshko doesn't sound Siberian."

"We're Ukes. That's where the name comes from. My grandfather, may he rest in peace, came from the Ukraine. And that's where the Siberian Poleshkos started."

The sun set and the earth cooled gradually. The steppe was plunged into warm darkness; the air was moist and smelled of fresh-cut grass.

Poleshko lit a campfire and the women, having washed up the bowls and spoons from supper, gathered around it like moths to a flame. Poleshko and I—the men—were closest to the fire. Poleshko poked the fire with a branch and squinted at the bright sparkles, his face gathered into wrinkled folds. Every evening he talked in his hoarse, smoker's voice, always about the same thing. He spoke unhurriedly, with long pauses and unnecessary details, about how he served before the Revolution in Saint Petersburg in the life guards, a crack corps with a height requirement of at least five feet ten inches. And once, near Saint Petersburg, he personally saw the tsar. Every time, they asked him, What did the tsar look like? And he replied unvaryingly, "What? You know what a tsar is. Head of the whole empire."

His answer did not make much sense, but no one asked any further questions.

The moon was a copper semicircle with dark spots above the edge of the steppe. It kept growing, swelling, tearing itself away from the earth, until it hung suspended, a full red sphere, lighting up the nearby clouds. A bird began singing, as if it had been waiting for the moon to rise. Off to one side I could just make out the outlines of the horses. They were let out to graze, but they never went far from the campfire.

Poleshko grew silent. It was time for the songs. The women sang softly and in the kind of harmony that comes from singing the same songs over and over again.

I had my own favorites. I listened to them with joy. Most of all, an old song touched me, a song I had never heard before Siberia and this village.

> Khaz-Bulat the brave,
> Your saklia is poor.
> I'll shower you with gold.
> I'll give you a steed, a knife,
> I'll give you my gun.
> And for all that
> Give me your wife.

The song must have come to Siberia from the Caucasus Mountains, for it was only there, as I remembered from my books, that a house was called a *saklia* and a man would have a non-Russian name like Khaz-Bulat.

> You are old and you are gray.
> It's no life for her with you.
> You will destroy the life
> Of your young and tender wife.

It was a long song, and the women loved the part about her wasted youth and fading beauty.

"Hey, girls, wouldn't it be fine to have a man," Rayka Gololobova said, stretching sweetly and spreading her strong arms, as her thick blond braid rose on her large breasts.

"Cut it out, you hot wench," Poleshko said, narrowing his eyes in disapproval. "You've got nothing but mischief on your mind."

"Some mischief with you," Rayka responded without malice, still stretching. "Lordy, if we at least had one man among us. One's too old, the other's not old enough. When our men get back, if they do, our beauty and youth will be gone."

"Shut up," Poleshko grumbled. "Let them sing."

I watched the women and thought how hard it was for them without husbands. At night I could hear their sighs, and sometimes even their weeping.

I felt better than I had in a long time. I was well fed and treated kindly. All twenty-six women were like mothers to me. No one lectured me. I was my own boss and I had my horse, shaggy Orlik, who carried me easily in the saddle over the tall, thick grass of the endless steppe.

But once a week my heart grew glum. I would canter into the village of Orlik, which my horse was named after, to turn in a report on the mown and racked hay. And it wasn't the fact that the report was a lie that bothered me—I doubled the figures so the women could earn a little something. No one checked up on me, and they wouldn't notice until winter when they hauled the hay to the farm. By then my tracks would be cold, as I wasn't planning to stay long. But hearing the distant train horn, I grew tense and jittery. I was beginning to miss the dreamy *clickety-clack* of the wheels, the smoky wind, and the constantly shifting pictures on either side of the speeding train.

Something else ruined my mood. Every time I headed back to the steppe, I was given a thin packet of letters in triangular military envelopes. I delivered them to my women.

More than half my brigade was made up of widows, who had already received death notices. But the ones with living husbands at the front or in the hospital counted every hour and stared at the horizon to catch a glimpse of me, waiting with bated breath to see if I would make them happy or sad.

One time I brought only two letters. One I gave to curly-haired Rayka Gololobova, I held on to the other one—it was official. Rayka couldn't open the letter for a long time, her fingers wouldn't obey, and when she did, and read it, her cracked lips moving, she shouted in a high, piercing, joyous cry:

"He's alive, Vasya is! He's in the hospital!"

The other women were like dark statues along the stack, their heads and faces covered with kerchiefs to shield them from the sun. They had nothing to wait for. Each had received a burial notice for her husband. They couldn't share her joy. They were silent, leaning on their pitchforks and rakes. Their silence was sullen and bitter.

"What about me, foreman?"

Skinny, short Pasha Ovchinnikova stood by Orlik's head. Her husband had left her with four children when he went off to war. Pasha's face was withered and wrinkled, and when she spoke to me her gnarled fingers pulled the edge of the kerchief away from her lips. In her colorless eyes quivered fear, and her sun-bleached lashes trembled.

This was the hardest moment. The official letter was for her, Pasha Ovchinnikova, and to spare her, I had planned to give it to her later, after work. But she was asking for it, and without looking up, I handed her the thin envelope. I pulled on Orlik's reins and rode away. Pasha's thin howl pierced my back. She fell facedown into the hay and kicked and cried like a funeral mourner. The other women wept with her.

My Orlik shook his head in fear, and I began coughing to cover up my need to cry.

I let them cry themselves out. When it started to quiet down, I rode over to Ovchinnikova, got down from my horse, and bent over her.

153

"Pasha? Hey, Pasha? You go home. Hear?"

I helped the tear-stained and sobbing Pasha get up on Orlik and slapped his back. The horse gave me a surprised look with his round eye and went off, swaying the downcast Pasha in the saddle. The women, wiping their eyes with their fingers, watched her go.

"Enough!" I said, waving my arm. "Let's get back to work!"

I picked up Pasha's pitchfork and climbed up on the stack. The women smiled at me through their tears. Trying to distract them, I began shouting:

"Come on, girls, come on! Everything for the front, for victory!"

That slogan callused your eyes wherever you went. Everything for the front, for victory. And I couldn't come up with anything better to cheer on my women.

The dry, sun-baked hay crumbled, fell behind my collar, and stuck to my wet shoulder blades, prickling and tickling. I worked furiously, tossing huge chunks of hay with the pitchfork. The women caught them, placed them on the stacks, and trampled them down with bare feet. The stack was springy. It looked as if they were dancing and shaking their pitchforks. We worked without stop, without a break, to dull the grief with exhaustion—no thinking, no feeling. Just wave the pitchforks and trample the hay, layer after layer.

I also went into the village for food with Lyubka Saltaeva, the cook's assistant. We were issued grain, onions, salt, cooking oil, and big loaves of bread. The bread was strictly rationed, and when I got back to the group, I measured out each woman's weekly portion.

Lyubka Saltaeva was the youngest in the brigade, if you didn't count me. She wasn't sixteen yet.

Lyubka was a sturdy Siberian lass, with gray eyes. Her eyebrows were bleached by the sun to the color of straw, just like her straight hair, which was pulled back into a tight bun. Her cheekbones were prominent—Siberians have a lot of Asiatic blood. Despite the kerchief she used to cover her face, her perky nose was mercilessly burned and peeled like a new potato.

Once we picked up the food, we spent the night in the village—Lyubka stayed at her parents' house and I slept in the hayloft of the stables—and started out in the morning. We took the wooden barrel out of the wagon, put down several planks on the frame, piled up hay on top, and sat back to back with our legs dangling—me on one side, Lyubka on the other.

Of all the women, Lyubka was the least noticeable. She kept quiet when the women started talking frankly and shamelessly around the fire. I hadn't even paid any attention to her before this trip. It was a long way back. And there wasn't much you could talk about with Lyubka. She replied in monosyllables, without looking up. She was shy of me, the foreman, even though I was a good eighteen months younger. But I was tall and strong for my age.

The wagon rolled along the ruts of the road through wheat fields still green with a silvery tint—a sign that the sheaves were filling in. Bearded barley was turning golden—the first to go under the blades of the thresher.

Fattened gophers clumsily ran across the road. A lark floated in the air above the grain, as if suspended by an invisible thread, beating its wings and whistling its heart out, trilling with joy.

The village was far behind us, and now we were surrounded by the even steppe.

"Have you ever kissed?" I burst out for no reason.

"Sez you," Lyubka said, her neck turning red.

I was becoming aroused by women for the first time in my life. But they didn't consider me a man. I occasionally caught someone giving me a dreamy come-hither look, but when my eyes met it, it was turned off. The women were dying for men. They were young and healthy—beautiful, all of them. However, not one woman ever hinted to me, beckoned me, ever thought to seduce me on the sly from the others. It must have been the moral rectitude of the village. It grew harder and harder for me to remain a eunuch. I caught myself watching the women excitedly. I liked them all.

At sunset, when work on the steppe was over, the women stopped at the brook, at the spot where there was a deep hollow and the water fell in a heavy warm stream. Behind the waterfall a small pond had formed. They bathed there, pulling off their dusty shirts and skirts, they splashed naked, sitting in a circle in the shallow water. We didn't have soap, and the women scrubbed each other with silt from the river bottom. They rinsed off under the waterfall.

I could barely control myself as I lay on my belly and looked at the white firm bodies of the women, laughing, pushing each other under the waterfall. Their loosened braids were wet and stuck to their shoulders, backs, and breasts. Streams fell down their rolling hips and rounded bellies. I stared until they came out of the water and got dressed—that was the signal for me to get out of there, and I crawled like a snake to my horse.

My peeking remained a secret from them all. But old Poleshko, I don't know how, found out and said to me once as he hammered out the blade of a mower:

"You're behaving badly, foreman. You'll lose your authority."

I didn't ask him, pretending innocence of what he was talking about, but I stopped going near the waterfall when they were bathing.

Orlik was the first to sense the nearness of the brook. He was thirsty, and scenting the water, he neighed. Our camp was a stone's throw from there. I could see smoke rise to the sky—dinner was waiting for us.

It grew as dark as twilight, even though it was just after noon. To the east, where you could make out distant blue hills, a thundercloud was forming, quickly spreading over the sky. A storm was coming and we urged on the horse, hoping to get back to the camp dry. Two sacks of bread and grain were in the back. Thunder grumbled behind us.

The road crossed the brook near the waterfall. The wheels rattled on the stones, splashing. And the rain lashed down heavily. We were soaked to the skin in a minute. Lyubka and I hopped under the wagon, trying to protect the food sacks.

The thunder and lightning cracked the sky above our heads. The water made its way through the hay and planks and dropped onto our backs in warm streams. The wagon wasn't high. We had to crouch under it, our heads bumping the planks, our foreheads practically touching.

Lyubka's gray eyes were just at my eyebrows. I could have licked her peeling nose with a drop dangling from its tip. I could see two breasts close to her chin, showing in relief under her wet shirt. They rose and fell. Lyubka breathed deep and often. I must have been panting too. Later, everything that I did and what she did got all mixed up in my memory. We fell on our sides. The rain lashed at our heads and feet. I tore the wet clothes off her and she tore off mine. I remember her slippery wet body, her lips, and her moan, prolonged and high-pitched. There we lay side by side in the water. Our overheated bodies were bathed by the rain. The thunder still rolled over the wagon, as if a tractor were squashing it. From the front came the sharp smell of horse manure. Either fear or happiness had made Orlik drop a steaming load onto the ground.

The storm was soon blown farther along with the ragged clouds, and the sky, washed clean to a sparkling blue, showed a pale rainbow. Lyubka and I climbed out from under the wagon. The sacks of bread were soaked, and we pulled out the loaves one after another to dry on the straw.

"Let's go for a swim!" I pulled Lyubka to the waterfall.

She looked around to see if anyone was there. Then, with a squeal, she jumped under the waterfall with me. The water broke on our heads. We bumped elbows, bellies, and backs. We shouted, leaped, and splashed.

We returned to the camp about two hours later. Dozens of sharp, all-noticing eyes were watching us from all the tents. Our bewildered faces must have given us away. Looking busy and frowning, I un-hitched Orlik, trying to keep my back to the tents. Lyubka unloaded the sacks and stared at the ground as if she were searching for something.

"Congratulations!" Rayka Gololobova cried from her tent. "Sillies! What are you hiding your eyes for? It's your day today! And we old women can merely admire you."

She kept muttering without knowing the truth of what she said. Rayka was twenty-two. And she was a widow, even though she didn't know it yet. Lyubka and I knew. The letter was damp in my pocket.

Rayka winked at Lyubka and me, and said, "We should drink to this occasion, eh, girls? But the trouble is we don't have anything to drink. That damn war!"

Part III

11

Once again I was filthy. Once again my clothes were worn to tatters. The elbows and knees of my clothes gaped with ragged holes that my crusty body showed through.

I earned food by singing on trains and at over-crowded railroad stations. Even though times were still hungry, and small amounts of food were available only through ration cards, I was able to survive. A soft-hearted peasant woman might give me half her baked potato, or a man after some hesitation might offer me the uneaten portion of his homemade pie. The most generous were soldiers on trains headed for the front and invalids making their way home from hospitals. They would give me such riches as bread, or half a tin of canned meat, or a lump of sugar.

163

Basically, I wasn't starving, most of the time. And I was free to travel wherever I wanted. Sometimes westward with the soldiers, sometimes eastward with the mangled tanks and guns that were being shipped to the Urals for repairs.

It was the hot summer of 1943, a watershed in the war. The Germans were being chased out of Russia. The war rolled westward, freeing occupied territories one after the other, thereby revealing open wounds—burned-out villages, ruins of cities, destroyed military equipment by the sides of the road.

Now trains of civilians were heading west, back home, instead of east. People who had fled their homes were coming back to their ruined houses. When I came across trains like that, my spirits fell. I remembered my mother and sister. My last memory of them was of my sister's back and feet, my mother holding her close to her lap. She was trying to protect her from the German plane that was howling its way right at us from the dark night sky.

We were sitting with some other people on the open flatcars of a train that was running away from the German planes. It was the very beginning of the war—the third night.

The bomb exploded next to the moving train, just as our car went by, and I was blown off by the shock wave. I did have time to see Mother's frozen face with its mouth open and to note this detail—my sailor cap had fallen from my head into her hand. And I thought, or maybe I just imagined it, that the cap would be the only thing Mama would have to remember me by.

Because she had nothing else to remind her that she ever had a son, not even a picture.

The train rushed past into the dark to the distant glow of a burning station. I stayed on the side of the tracks alive and well. My mother and sister disappeared, swallowed into the distant, burning glow.

Now, two years later, I was watching trains go by carrying people returning home. I peered into women's faces in the crazy, futile hope for a miracle. But as they taught us at school, miracles don't happen. They were invented by the church to fool uneducated people. I was educated, and so I couldn't even hope.

I was fifteen, tall and thin, but as strong and resilient as a horse. Skin and bones, and between them sinews, hard as rope. Once a woman who had listened to me sing at a station said pityingly:

"He should be getting married instead of begging for food."

"How do you suggest I feed myself?" I wanted to shout. "Rob you, you old fool? Earning bread by singing isn't the worst thing in the world."

And it was singing that determined my future.

I was in a small station on the Upper Volga called Glotovka, performing my standard repertoire of pop hits of the period—"The Girl Sees the Soldier Off to War," "Black Night—Only Bullets Whizzing Past," and "They Took Her Away to a Life of Shame, Her Tender Hands Bound." The soldiers, most of them not young, listened with softening faces, and I watched with practiced eye for the moment when they would start blinking sentimentally, to switch to my patter:

"Kind folk! The war took my parents. I'm an orphan. I'm alone, unfed and thirsty. I haven't had a bite in three days. Give me what you can."

Usually the soldiers frowned grimly to hide their tears and felt around in their pockets. But this particular time they didn't get a chance to pull anything out. They were stopped by a command:

"Halt! Come on, let me have a look at this eagle."

The soldiers stepped aside hurriedly, letting through a tall and stocky officer, his jacket unbuttoned over his stomach, revealing a purple knit undershirt. His green shoulder boards showed two blanks and three large stars: a colonel, the commander of these soldiers and the guns. His cap with the black patent-leather visor was casually pushed back, exposing bushy brows, teasing eyes, and the mocking, sleek look of a man spoiled by power. I cringed, expecting nothing good from our encounter.

"You sing?"

All I could do was nod.

"What else can you do?"

I thought and shrugged, trying to figure out what he was leading up to and what problems the question could bring.

"Do you know poetry?"

That confused me completely, but I nodded.

"Can you recite?"

I nodded slightly.

"Let's see," the colonel said, giving a sneaky look to the left and right at his soldiers, who were respectfully smiling at him. "And if you're lying, we'll turn you over to the military patrol. Got it? Do you know 'The Dnieper is marvelous in fine weather'?"

" 'The Dnieper is marvelous' isn't a poem," I said glumly. "It's prose. By the great Russian writer Gogol."

"Oh-ho!" the colonel gasped. "You know that! You're not a faker. Go on, recite it, if you know it."

Luckily, I remembered a couple of lines from that piece, which we had studied in school before the war.

I cleared my throat, spread my legs, and put my hands behind my back—the sleeves came up to my elbows. I had to please that eccentric man, or I would end up in the hands of the military police.

"The Dnieper is marvelous in fine weather," I declaimed, "when it rolls its waters freely."

It flowed on and on, as if a source had sprung up in my brain. Not only the colonel, but all the men listened, mouths agape.

When I stopped, the colonel shook his head like a horse and spoke in a different, warmer voice.

"Not bad, tramp! Who are you?"

"An orphan," I said humbly.

"Who were your parents?"

"Military."

"Father's rank?"

"Like you. But they didn't wear shoulder boards then. It was before the war."

"He had four bars?"

"Yes. He was commander of a cavalry-artillery division."

"Did he die?"

167

I nodded.

"Listen," the colonel decided. "Come with us. You shouldn't be hanging around stations begging for handouts. You'll be 'son of the regiment.' Understand?"

And immediately he gave orders.

"Wash him! Dress him. And bring him to me."

I still hadn't figured out what had happened, but the soldiers, gabbing happily, had already led me to the station pump, stripped me, and set me under the stream of cold water that flowed from the tall pipe used to fill up steam engines. They scrubbed the crusted dirt from my skin. They cut my shaggy hair. They found a shirt, hemmed some jodhpurs, located boots that fit; and by the time the train left Glotovka, I was standing before the colonel in his train compartment. He, delighted by my transformation, said with satisfaction, "A youth in his prime!"

That phrase became my name. Colonel Galemba did not like my Jewish name, and he always referred to me as the youth in his prime.

He gave me delicious food I had never seen before. Canned American pork, scrambled eggs made from American powdered eggs, and sweet, strong tea.

I relaxed, drowsy from the food. Trying not to fall asleep, I listened to the colonel as he told me how he had lost his family—a wife and daughter. The girl was almost my age, a year older. They didn't evacuate in time and were lost without a word.

"Do you want me to adopt you? Eh? You and I will be a family."

I didn't reply because I was asleep. Sitting up, leaning against the wall, my head dropped on my chest. In my sleep, I felt someone lay me down on the seat and put something very, very soft under my head.

When we reached our destination, Colonel Galemba announced that I was his son and moved me into his quarters.

In the apartment where we were billeted, he attached a zinc basin to the wall by the door. It was filled almost to the brim not with water, but with pure alcohol spirits. Every morning the colonel scooped out a half glass and gulped it down straight on an empty stomach. And he taught me to do it.

"Youth in his prime!" He would wake me. "Rise and shine!"

I drank with my eyes shut, holding my breath, coughing and spluttering. He would laugh and slap my back, saying, "You're turning into a man. But we won't let you become a drunk. We'll stop you when it's time. Drinking isn't mandatory, but knowing how to drink is. Otherwise, what kind of a man are you? As your father, I'll have to watch out for you. You won't shame your father, will you, son? Youth in his prime!"

Every day he grew more attached to me, and tried to keep me nearby. As soon as I set off somewhere, I'd hear, "Youth in his prime!"

We were stationed in a village, preparing to move out to our battle position. The colonel and I had a whole house, abandoned by its owners. It was a hot summer. To get away from the heat, my fat "father" liked to lie down at noon in his underwear on the cool floor. He liked me to lie down perpendicular to him and shake his big belly with my bare feet.

It was fun, and I enjoyed mauling his belly with my toes, as he groaned with pleasure and said:

"Just like a family! Isn't it?"

12

The colonel's regiment was not the usual artillery regiment, but a special one, brought into battle only in the most extraordinary circumstances. We had heavy antiaircraft guns, but instead of planes, we shot at tanks at close range—with direct aim.

In normal battle circumstances guns are aimed using sights, but direct aim uses no accessories, just pointing the barrel in a straight line at the target and allowing the target to get as close as possible. Our artillery men sometimes let tanks get within twenty yards before shooting, without even aiming. They never missed. A shot like that would knock the turret off the tank. But tanks have guns and machine guns— and our gunners left themselves open. After one shot or at best two, they were destroyed themselves. Therefore after every battle only the horns and hoofs, so to speak, were left of the regiment—no more than a quarter of the men, and none of the guns, survived. The arithmetic was simple: For each enemy tank hit, almost the same number of guns were lost, hit for hit. But the enemy's attack was halted. The pathetic remains were brought back behind the lines to regroup and receive new equipment.

Our regiment went into battle rarely, only when there was a dangerous situation and it looked like the enemy would attack with tanks. Our command determined the direction of their main thrust, and that was where our regiment went under cover of night. We took our positions in the dark, setting up the guns, digging communication lines and foxholes, and waited for dawn, a last dawn for most of our men.

Our regiment's personnel changed endlessly. You could count the veterans who had been with us from the first battle on your fingers. There are some people who survive in places where it is impossible to survive. For some inexplicable reason bullets pass them by. And if they are hit, it's not mortally.

Samokhin had been through more than a dozen battles and was still alive when I was transferred to that battery. The coming battle was to be the first in my life. I reported to Captain Saulenko, the battery commander, about whom I remember only that he had short fat legs and his boots had to be split on top to accommodate his heavy calves; I reported, and I could tell from his worried face that he knew who I was to Colonel Galemba and that he expected nothing good to come of it. I took over for the battery's radioman, who had just been hospitalized. The equipment consisted of a field telephone in a green wooden box, a couple of dry batteries, and a heavy reel of cable. I used my short-handled sapper's shovel to dig in the sticky wet ground, burrowing out a niche in the foxhole wall where I could take cover.

The fog that morning spread like torn cotton batting over the wet meadow in front of the battery. Beyond the meadow, where you could see a church belfry, was the enemy. According to our intelligence, there were many tanks behind the village, which meant that the main thrust should be expected here. Our regiment would take the blow.

No one shut his eyes all night: The tanks might appear out of the fog at any minute. An hour before I arrived, the enemy tried to feel out our position with artillery fire. The regiment did not respond—we did not want to give away our positions.

Now the Germans shot sporadically, trying to get on our nerves. The foxhole was cold and damp—spring was late—and I warmed up by shoveling and setting up my simple household in the niche. I tested the line. The command point of the regiment did not respond. I started twirling the handle and shouting into the phone. Nothing but static came in response. Captain Saulenko came over, spread his fat legs in front of my face, hunched over the phone, and said wearily, "What are you shouting for? Communications are down. The line was cut by a shell."

That meant that I had to get out of the foxhole and crawl in the slimy meadow, in the cold water, holding on to the wire with one hand until I got to the spot where it was broken and connect the two ends. And then come back.

"Permission to go check the line?" I straightened.

"What will you check?" the captain said, chewing his lip sourly. "You'll get lost. . . . I'll have to answer for you."

The hint was clear. The captain knew who had adopted me.

"I'll go, Captain," came a voice with a cold from behind the captain. "Leave him. . . . He's new, and young."

I stretched to see who had stood up for me. He was sitting on an ammo box, hunched up like a village grandpa on a bench. He rolled a cigarette in a piece of newspaper, licking the edge to stick it together. He had a peasant's thin, tobacco-stained mustache and long yellow teeth like a horse's; deep wrinkles scored his face; and he had eyes as prickly as hedgehogs beneath bushy eyebrows. He was wearing a well-worn cotton jacket that had lost its former greenish color and had black scorch marks from sleeping near campfires. He also had faded trousers with raggedy patches on the knees, worn gray shoes, and puttees rising from them along his thin bony legs to his knees. A flattened hat with ear flaps hung over his brows. A hard-working soldier of the old school.

That's what he looked like the first time I saw him— my future mentor, Pavel Ivanovich Samokhin, private in the guards.

"Why should you do anything for him?" the captain

snorted, and squinted meanly at me. "Signing on as nanny, are you?"

"He's underage. . . . No wonder they call him the regimental son."

"Some regimental son. . . . Do you know whose son he is now? You're trying to please his father?"

"Who's his pappy?"

"You don't know?" the captain said, disbelieving. "Colonel Galemba adopted him. . . . Understand? And dumped him on us."

"Huh? Adopted him, eh?" Samokhin drawled. "Then let his father go out for him. Why don't you call HQ and tell that to the regiment commander." He stopped and looked up at the captain. "What's the matter, no guts? Cat got your tongue?"

Saulenko made a face. "I'm not afraid of anyone. They won't send me any farther than this. What do I care? I'll tell them. But how do I tell the colonel? The wire's down."

"Well, then I'll go fix it," Samokhin said, getting up with a groan, "and then you and the colonel can chat all you want."

"No, I'll go!" I said, jumping up.

"Sit." Samokhin shoved me aside with his elbow. "Where are your tools?"

He stuck a pair of pliers, a piece of wire, and a roll of electrical tape into his pocket and climbed up out of the foxhole. Samokhin didn't crawl, he walked, bent over, along the wire, letting it slip through his fist.

The captain and I watched him go. A shell flew overhead and exploded not far from Samokhin. He managed to hit the dirt, and then jumped up quickly after the explosion and went on his way.

The captain and I looked at each other.

"Next time you go yourself," the captain said. "Is that clear?"

"It's clear," I said, looking down.

"Maybe there won't be another time," Saulenko sighed. "We're going to feel the heat soon. Have you ever been in combat? We're dead men. A shitty father you've got . . . sending you into this hole."

The Germans decided not to attack that morning, and we hung around in battle readiness.

Samokhin fixed the line and returned to the battery. When he got back to me to return the tools, he asked:

"How old are you?"

"Fifteen," I said.

"God," sighed Samokhin. "Russia's really in bad shape. Sending children to be slaughtered."

Then he told me confidentially that I could rest easy. According to his observations, if the Germans didn't attack by dawn, they wouldn't move until the following day. They're a precise, punctual people. Samokhin had learned their tricks. So we could relax and not worry, save our strength.

We also talked about what had happened to my parents and how I managed without them, all alone in the world. We both decided that there were a few good people in the world. He also asked whether my adoptive father was treating me well and decided that the colonel was right in sending me to the battery; otherwise the regiment would be full of whispers that he was shielding his own, but putting others into danger.

"A smart man, with a head on his shoulders. Handsome. And in fine fettle," Samokhin said, evaluating my adoptive father. "You got lucky. He'll set you on the right path."

He began rolling a cigarette with clumsy stiff fingers. Giving me a sidelong glance, he said, as if in passing, "My fingers don't bend. They've had it. It's hard to hold a pencil. I'd like to write home. . . . Why put it off for tomorrow? . . . They might be writing death notices about us tomorrow."

I got his message and played along. "Let me write for you. You dictate, and I'll write it down."

"Really?" Samokhin didn't hide his pleasure. "You're quick. Well, let's do it."

Bent over, we climbed into the wet niche with my telephone equipment. I spread out a notebook on my lap while Samokhin sharpened my pencil with his knife.

"Where should we start?" mused Samokhin. "Well, start the right way. Write: A good day and a low bow to the whole family. To my father-in-law Grigori Isaich, to my wife Maria Feodrovna, and the children—Nikolai, Olga, Aleksander, Stepan, and . . . I've forgotten the fifth one. . . . Born after I left, christened without me. God grant me memory. I remember. Lizaveta. And now . . . in the first lines of my letter . . ."

I wasn't writing it down. I listened, pretending to move my pencil over the page. Samokhin couldn't see that—and he was carried away, transported home, near Penza, in his thoughts.

"I know that until the potato harvest, things are

tight for you. But how can I help? I'm far. We have nothing ourselves. The food rations are measured. Can't scrape up enough to send a food parcel home. So just bear up . . . a little bit more. The war won't last a century. . . . I'll come back and things will get better. As long as you have the bones, the meat will grow around them."

I listened to his muttering and saw how close he was to his family, how tenderly he loved them, and how he worried about them. He just couldn't find the right words.

I got the idea to write down everything Samokhin was suffering and couldn't express. I began writing as if I were an adult and writing home to my family: to my beloved wife and dear children.

"Well, read what you've scribbled there," Samokhin asked, seeing that I had finished writing.

I began reading in a hoarse whisper, my voice breaking. Samokhin, rolling a smoke, stopped in midroll.

"My dear, darling Masha!"

That's how I started the letter.

"My dearest children . . ."

And I named each one not with their dry adult names, but with diminutive pet names . . . Kolenka, Olechka, Sashenka, Stepochka, and my tiny, adorable Lizanka.

In my opinion that was how a loving father and husband had to address his family.

I took a breath and glanced over at Samokhin. He sat without moving, giving me a nasty, suspicious look.

The letter ended with these words:

"The long-awaited victory will come. We will destroy the enemy and I will return to my hearth and press you to my soldier's bosom, and there will be no one happier than us in the whole wide world."

I stopped. My tongue was furry and my mouth dry. I looked at Samokhin guiltily and saw that the prickly hedgehogs had melted in his eyes, which were filled with tears. He sniffed and spat angrily:

"You're a fine liar!"

And then concluded:

"It'll make the old woman bawl!"

I mailed the letter myself.

Samokhin grew attached to me, even though he tried not to show it. I knew that I satisfied his longing for his own children, whom he hadn't seen since the war began.

I loved sleeping next to him. On the ground, in the foxholes, in the rain, he always managed to set up a "human" sleeping arrangement, as he called it. He wouldn't lie on bare dirt. He would always find pine branches or hay and make a soft and dry place. He would set up my reel of cable at the head, softening the sharp edges with a quilted vest and our caps. We covered ourselves with our greatcoats, and Samokhin tucked me in so that I wouldn't get cold in my sleep. He'd smoke his bedtime cigarette, waving the smoke away from my face, and talking to me in a hoarse smoker's voice, coughing and spitting.

"Never, you hear me, never rush around . . . people. There is nothing worse than a bustling man. That means he wants something at someone else's expense. Well, if he's as direct as a sword . . . that's no good, either. The best is the golden mean. Say you're going into battle. . . . Don't rush out first . . . don't be pushy. People don't like that. But bullets do. They find fools fast. And it's not right to be among the last either. They'll laugh at you, give you no respect. And the bullets will find you too . . . not the enemy's, but ours.

"So, little soldier, remember what I say, stick to the middle. . . . You'll be protected from front and back.

"Or, for another example, swearing. . . . Swearing, swearing, swearing . . . People can't talk like humans. They swear on their mothers . . . and curse mothers right and left. . . . But you have only one mother.

"That word should be respected like something holy. . . . When death comes, who does the soldier call for? His mother . . . not his father . . . not his wife, his mother. I saw enough of that in the hospital. A man may have gray in his beard, but when he's dying, he whispers 'Mama.' So you be like that. . . . Don't follow the example of fools. . . . Don't defile your tongue. Mother swearing is like an ulcer, brother, it eats into you. . . . You won't be able to wash it off the rest of your life."

My language had been fouled back in the orphanages and trade schools, and when I was in the army, I really let loose, trying to cover up my tender years with rough salty language.

Samokhin was probably the only man in the whole unit who didn't curse, and around him the others swore less. Curses flew from my lips on their own, and every time I saw Samokhin, I bit my tongue, but the curses still slipped out. In his eyes I saw compassion, not condemnation.

It was hard for me to watch my language for another

180

reason. My adoptive father, Colonel Galemba, was a terrible curser. He was a virtuoso. He loved starting a lengthy, convoluted tirade that included God, the cross, your mother, and everything else that came to mind. Using his rich actor's voice, he readily swore in front of his subordinates, thinking it made him more democratic, closer to the simple folk.

He did not control his tongue around me, and I kept up with him, using my orphanage vocabulary.

"What, what did you say?" he asked delightedly, hearing a new curse. "Come now, repeat it. . . . Got it. Fine. Wonderful. Excellent." And he repeated the words, relishing them, and liked me all the more.

"Whatever you say, we're a great nation. Where else are there curses like that? With such fire, such thunder. The Germans? A joke. They can't catch up with us. That's why they can't beat us. They don't have our guts."

When we were away from the front, I left the unit, or rather what remained of it after combat, and moved back in with Colonel Galemba. Usually he was quartered in the best of the surviving houses, and I switched to the easy civilian life while I was there. Samokhin remained, like the other soldiers, in a barracks situation. He missed me. When he had a pass, he spent his hours hanging around the commander's house in hope of seeing me. And as soon as I saw his bent, bony frame in the worn uniform, I would race out into the street and spend with him all the leave time he had.

Then the regiment would start preparing for new battles, and I would leave the comfort and food of the commander's quarters to return to Samokhin and the regiment.

Our soldiers took their revenge in Germany—for all the hardships of the war, for the blood and the tears, for the grief the Germans brought to Russia in their pillaging and burning.

The hour of revenge had come. And the authorities did not interfere. The soldiers burst into houses, stuffing whatever they could get their hands on into sacks. Whatever they couldn't carry—say, mirrors, crystal chandeliers, porcelain—they shot up with their submachine guns, leaving showers of broken glass on the floor.

Watches were highly prized—wristwatches and pocket watches. Watches were hard to come by in Russia then. They were expensive and rarely for sale.

Germans knew about the Russian penchant for watches and, as soon as they became prisoners, took off the watches and handed them over to the victors. Some soldiers had a half dozen watches on each arm, from wrist to elbow. Watches became a form of money. People traded cigarettes and vodka for watches. You could get anything for a watch.

I had never had a watch. And I couldn't grab one from a frightened German. But once I almost became the owner of two watches at the same time.

Samokhin and I were making our way through a ravine, dragging heavy shells tied to our backs. There was no other way of getting ammunition to the battery because of spring flooding and a blown-up bridge. Transportation was at a standstill. The shells had to be carried.

I was in front and came across a body. It was one of our soldiers, lying in the mud with outflung arms. A watch gleamed on each hand. Samokhin caught up with me and saw what I was looking at.

"What are you staring for? Never seen a watch before? And I thought you were a decent human. You're going to strip a dead man?"

I said that the dead man had no need of a watch, and we could get some use out of them.

"Forget it," Samokhin said curtly. "They sent us for ammunition, not to grandma's house for goodies."

We moved on, pulling our boots from the sucking mud with difficulty. Samokhin, gasping for air with his smoker's lungs, tried to console me.

"I wouldn't take a watch like that for free. That's no watch. It would tick for a while and then you'd have to throw it away."

"Would you have taken a good watch?" I smart-mouthed.

Samokhin took a few steps and then replied.

"If a good man gave it to me, why not? But who's going to give me one? What have I done to deserve it?"

And when we reached the battery, he added, as if in conclusion; "Once you soil a person's soul, you'll never get it clean."

13

A rumor spread through the army, soon confirmed—we would be allowed to send home from Germany one parcel no heavier than twenty-two pounds. The news excited the troops. Many soldiers had families at home living at a near-starvation level with nothing but rags to wear.

Samokhin was really excited. His large family near Penza was trying to eke out an existence. And now for the first time in his four years he had a chance to do something for them. But Samokhin would not take anything that did not belong to him. And how much could he save from his rations?

We were lucky once—we got to a food warehouse before any other soldiers. Samokhin was stunned by the mountains of canned food and looked at the colored labels suspiciously.

"Read what it says, so we don't pick up any garbage by accident. They say they eat frogs."

"The French eat frogs, not the Germans," I tried to convince him.

"You know everything," Samokhin said, obviously not satisfied. "The Germans have robbed all of Europe. They could have picked up some frogs from the French. Read carefully."

I read the labels by syllables, while he muttered impatiently: "Look for meat. Beef. Pork wouldn't be bad either. My family hasn't seen meat during the whole war."

I picked out two dozen cans, basing my choices not on the words but the pictures. Cows and pigs looked at me from the labels.

Samokhin packed it all in his bag and went looking for the field post office, to send it off to his village. That evening he returned, looking depressed.

"Did you mail it?" I asked.

"What was there to mail?" Samokhin said with his back to me. "An empty bag?"

"You lost it on the road?" I couldn't believe it. "You were robbed?"

"Listen!" He turned to me. "Spit into my eyes. I'm a lousy father. And there's no forgiving me."

From his rambling explanations, I discovered what had happened. Along the way to the post office he had met a column of prisoners just liberated from a concentration camp—emaciated, like skeletons. Samokhin looked at them, struggled with himself, and then opened his pack and gave them the food.

We got another package ready. Twenty-two

pounds, just what the regulations permitted, but we didn't have time to take it to the post office. The front moved forward unexpectedly. We went out twice into direct fire.

The building our soldiers took for billeting was whole. Even the windowpanes were in place. It was empty, not a live German on any of the floors. But everything stood where it was supposed to in the apartments, as if the owners had gone out for a second and would be right back.

A half hour later the place was in shambles. Finally getting some leave, and having looked death in the face, the soldiers went wild on every floor. They opened all the wardrobes, tried on clothes for laughs, and ran from apartment to apartment to visit one another in pajamas and even women's nightgowns.

Samokhin didn't go looking for a place to sleep upstairs where the expensive apartments were. And he didn't let me, either.

"The officers will come," he said, "and chase everyone away. But nobody will want what we have."

Beneath the marble staircase was a narrow door, and Samokhin figured out that that was the servants' quarters.

"That's just for us," he said, opening the unlocked door.

We went into a small and very cozy apartment—a kitchen and two rooms: the dining room and the bedroom. By German standards a poor apartment—when we first got to Germany, we slept in houses that were much wealthier. But the luxury in this poor apartment was more than Samokhin could ever dream of in his village near Penza. And even I, the son of a division commander, never saw anything in any of our military apartments like what we found in the German servants' place.

Mounds of porcelain dishes and sterling silver with dull sheen stood in a glass hutch. The furniture was upholstered and made of walnut. The kitchen was finished with blue tiles the likes of which I had never seen. Rows of colored canisters stood on the shelves, and each was labeled in Gothic writing—salt, pepper, sugar, and many others I did not know.

"It's so clean, you don't want to sit anywhere," Samokhin said, scratching the back of his head.

We were filthy—straight from combat. We stank of sweat like overworked horses. Our boots were caked with mud and our nails were lined with black dirt.

"Don't make a mess. Understand?" Samokhin warned me, taking his green pack from his back.

"Well, it's like this. We don't know how long we'll be here. Only the top brass knows that. Let's at least have a decent meal."

He held a sooty kettle with dented sides by its aluminum handle. The kettle was full almost to the brim with borsch with a good beef bone sticking out—our dinner, which he had picked up at the field kitchen. An aluminum spoon stuck out from his boot top. I carried my spoon, with a shortened handle, in my shirt pocket—it was cleaner there, and we rarely had a chance to wash our spoons before eating.

The round table was covered with a fringed green velvet cloth. Samokhin didn't want to set the dirty ̶ ̶ ̶ ̶ ̶ ̶ ̶ ̶ e tablecloth, so he put it down on the floor by his chair. He sat in an armchair, leaned on the velvet tablecloth, smiled, pushing apart his wrinkles, and said, enjoying himself: "And now you can serve me. You're young, and my old bones need a rest. You be the waiter, like I've come to a restaurant. Eat your fill. We don't need anything fancy. Just some soldier's borsch. Set the table. Don't drop the dishes. Bring everything we need. Forks, spoons, knives. And salt, pepper . . . what else? You've been to restaurants, I bet. You must know."

I placed a flat porcelain plate with a gold rim in front of him, and a matching bowl on top. I gave him a spoon, fork, and knife from the large set kept behind glass. I set a place for me. I brought salt and pepper in porcelain shakers from the kitchen. And I pranced around the table like a servile waiter.

"Now it's my turn," Samokhin said, joining in the game. He took the ladle from me and poured the borsch neatly into the bowls, shouting sternly:

"Don't squirm!"

The borsch made my mouth water, and it was all I could do to keep from drooling on the tablecloth as I sat down.

"Godspeed! Let's go!" Samokhin ordered, pulling his chair closer, and when I looked up at him, I almost spat out my first spoonful of the soup.

My old man was so excited that he had forgotten about the silverware shimmering on the green cloth. He had automatically pulled out his aluminum spoon from his boot and was slurping away.

No sooner had we had a bit of soup than the kitchen

door slammed and we heard voices: a woman and children. They were babbling in German, and from the way Samokhin was frozen with his spoon, I could tell that they were in the dining room. I turned and saw three people: a rather young woman and two children, a boy and girl. The strips of their heavy backpacks dug into their shoulders. The woman was carrying a heavy brown suitcase.

"The owners are back," Samokhin said, and was as embarrassed as if they had caught him doing something vile: He had broken into someone's house without permission. "Well, come in. Why stand around? Come and sit."

He spoke to them in Russian, not realizing that they couldn't understand. He half rose on his bandy legs, looking as if he were offering them his place at the table.

"*Bitte,*" I said in German, thereby exhausting a large part of my vocabulary.

A smile crossed the woman's pale face, and her children smiled at us meekly.

"Call her to the table!" Samokhin ordered me. "What's the matter? Cat got your tongue? The people must be hungry from their trip."

I became a witness to a most curious sight. The people, who didn't know a word of Russian, guessed exactly what Samokhin said, just by his intonation and gestures. Obviously human kindness sounds the same in any language and does not need translation.

He and I noticed at the same time that the children had their hungry eyes on our bowls of soup and the

189

mound of sliced bread on a plate in the middle of the table.

"That's it—come to the table!" ordered Samokhin, and he didn't have to repeat it. The children rushed to the glassed hutch for plates, but their mother stopped them. They put down the plates and reluctantly headed for the kitchen. The water ran—they were washing hands under their mother's supervision. All three returned to the dining room, their backpacks and coats off, and they sat down at the table with their plates. There was enough borsch for only one bowl.

"You don't want to eat from our bowls. We've dipped our mustaches in them," Samokhin said, scratching his chin in consternation. "However, you won't go without food."

He bent over the couch and, frowning and cursing, began undoing his pack with the food for his parcel.

"One can won't solve the problem," I heard him mutter.

He used his knife to open a long can of pork and dumped the pink chunk of meat onto the girl's plate.

"Share it with your brother!"

Then he looked around the table and said with a sigh, "Maria will forgive me. If you're the host, then you're the host. Why be cheap?"

A second can appeared from his sack. Smaller, with a cow on the label. He opened it and shook out a rounded cylinder of beef.

"With pepper!" he said, praising his goods. "And bay leaf!" And he sat down.

Only then did the woman and children start eating. I got back to my borsch. Samokhin ate slowly. As the host and the eldest at the table, he looked to make sure that everyone was happy. And so Samokhin fell into a philosophical mood and began musing aloud.

"And why did you push this war on us? Don't you have enough? You've got plenty, enjoy it and live. No, you wanted other people's things too. And what happened? You brought on your own misfortune, not to mention ours. Total ruination. I have five children of my own. Their stomachs have suffered. They'd be happy to see a potato. If they were at this table and each one had a serving of meat—they'd swallow it plate and all. Ah, why talk about it! It's just damn lousy!"

And he added: "Forgive the language."

I almost fell down laughing.

The woman listened to his thoughts in a foreign language and nodded, agreeing with everything and smiling shyly. That just egged him on and he kept talking.

"Let her eat," I said.

"You think you know everything," Samokhin said, miffed. But he shut up.

The children finished eating and wiped their plates with bread, then ran to the kitchen to wash them. The German woman said something I didn't understand. She went over to Samokhin, touched his filthy shirt, and showed, smiling shyly and rubbing her fists against each other, that she could wash it.

Samokhin was touched.

"It wouldn't be bad . . . you know . . . to have it washed. We never can—there's no time. We keep advancing and advancing, no end in sight."

He pulled his shirt off over his head and put it on his lap. He unscrewed his medals and decorations, laying each one on the green tablecloth. The children sprang up near the table and stared.

"What's to see?" Samokhin joked. "You have crosses, we have stars. Every nation amuses itself in its own way. There's a good saying: Whatever the child wants, as long as it stops crying."

Having removed everything from the shirt, he crumpled it up into a ball and handed it to the woman. She took it but didn't move. She put a finger on Samokhin's undershirt, offering to wash that too. It could have used a scraping—it was gray with sweat and dirt.

"What a pest! She'll have me naked," Samokhin said in embarrassment, but he submitted.

It was the first time I had seen him without a shirt. His body was white, but his hands and neck were dark brown, weathered by wind and sun as if they belonged to someone else and were just stuck on. His chest, stomach, and an upper arm were covered with sinuous scars from old wounds, and it looked as if his body had been repaired with a welding torch. Samokhin covered his chest like a woman by crossing his arms. His peasant dislike of being undressed before strangers was showing.

"Mistress," he called to the woman as she went off to the kitchen with his shirts and mine. "Do you have soap? Probably don't have a single piece, do you? Get some from my pack."

I opened his bag and took out two pieces of brown soap. I was about to put one back, but Samokhin stopped me.

"Give her both. One for the laundry. The other for her to have."

Now the boy and girl, feeling quite brave, surrounded half-naked Samokhin, examining his scars.

"What are you staring at? Counting the scars. You've studied geography in school, haven't you? That's Kharkov"—and he traced a scar on his stomach with his finger and then moved to his collarbone—"I got this in the Crimea. My arm is from Stalingrad."

The second he said Stalingrad the children's faces grew long and pitiful, as if they were about to cry. I followed their eyes and saw a portrait of a young man in German uniform. There was a funereal black ribbon tied to one corner of the frame. The woman stood in the doorway and also looked at the portrait. Tears were in her eyes. Everything was clear.

"Listen, mistress," Samokhin muttered. "Don't believe the notices. They often lie. It's quite possible that your man is alive. Stuck in prison, doing nothing! We took tons of prisoners there. Thousands!"

Soon our shirts and undershirts were hanging on a line stretched across the kitchen. The sight of drying laundry softened Samokhin up completely.

"We should pay her. After all, we're human. What do you think? If I leave a couple of cans, her feelings won't be hurt?"

193

He took two cans out from his pack and handed them to the children.

"Put them in the cupboard. Make your mother happy."

Our laundry wasn't fated to dry on the line. We heard tramping feet outside and the sergeant's hoarse voice rasped: "No more sleeping! Come out and line up!"

We were being transferred somewhere, and we rushed about the apartment getting ready for the road. We didn't put on the wet things. It was cold outside, early spring. We stuffed them in our packs. We put our quilted jackets over bare skin and pulled the belts tight. Samokhin scooped up the medals and decorations and stuck them in his pocket.

"Well, mistress, remember us kindly!" He shook her hand in farewell and went rummaging in his pack again, found a packet of sugar, handing it to the bewildered woman. "For the kids! All right! Good-bye!"

We ran along the courtyard, splashing in the dirty puddles. Our men were reluctantly getting into formation by the gate. Samokhin put his arms through his pack's straps and, as the half-empty bag hung on his back, he swore, looking away from me, "Damn! There goes my package home!"

14

"Youth in his prime," Colonel Galemba drawled, handing me a quarter-filled glass, "rise and shine."

Today my adoptive father was in fine form. Either because the German estate he had been quartered in pleased him or because of the heavy perfume of blooming cherry trees that fell into the window with its white damp clusters. The most likely reason, however, was that the warm spring air carried the smell of the end of the war. The town we were in for a brief rest lay on the outskirts of Berlin—the charred brick walls of the city metro station were just a half mile away.

The colonel had already put up his zinc basin filled with alcohol on the wall under a picture of the estate's owner, whose mustache bristled in a gilt carved frame, expressing his obvious dissatisfaction with the behavior of his uninvited guests. The living room was comfortable and cozy. My bare, long-suffering feet sank ankle deep in the carpet, the armchair enfolded my body softly and gently, and the black varnished side of the grand piano reflected my short hair and protruding ears.

"Drink to your future," the colonel said. "Here's some water . . . as a chaser."

He picked up a crystal carafe from the table and waited for me to drink so he could pour water in my glass.

Holding my breath, I drank the alcohol in one painless gulp. Water gurgled into the glass. I drank it down greedily, and my adoptive father's sleep-puffy face bent over me, spreading in a satisfied smile.

"Bravo! Good for you!"

He had already had a half glass before giving me mine, and now, carefully taking the glass, he put it back on the table next to the carafe and then silently paced back and forth on the fluffy carpet. He was only half dressed—he had his green jodhpurs, terry-cloth German slippers on his bare feet, and a purple knit undershirt unbuttoned on his white, hairless chest.

"That's it! The end of the war!" the colonel said, shaking his uncombed hair. "We made it, alive and well. Eh, son? Now we have to think how we'll live."

His nostrils flared nervously. His face was turning red.

"Eh, son?"

I saw that he liked calling me son. His eyes glowed. Something warm and very human showed in them.

"They'll sign the peace and shove me out of the army. A kick in the pants. Who needs me, an ignoramus? I'll be a general when I have a mule's ears. Well, who cares!"

I sat in the chair and turned my head from side to side following him around the living room. I felt safe and peaceful. To see my adoptive father like this, not buttoned up in a uniform, but half dressed, homey, was like family.

"Do you agree, son?"

"Yessir, comrade colonel!" I said with a smile.

"Drop that, you jerk! I'm talking to you like a son, and you . . ."

He leaned his head back with his eyes closed. This always preceded a recitation. The frustrated actor in the colonel was awakening.

"I'll settle on the shores of the Dnieper," he said without opening his eyes and whispering, "and I'll be a gooseherder. Wearing wide sharovary pants . . . and a straw hat . . . and I'll smoke a corncob pipe. . . . At one with nature. Just the geese honking . . . and suddenly! . . . What's that? A bell! I put my hand to my eyes . . . and I see dust on the road. The bell on the cart ring-a-dinging. . . . It's my son! From the university. Come to see his papa."

Opening his red-veined eyes, he burst into laughter and slapped my back.

"How's that? Like it? That's how it will be! Believe me. You'll go to the university, the first in our family, you'll be a graduate."

Without waiting for my reply, he walked to the window, shut his eyes again, and waved his right hand solemnly in the air.

"Like Lomonosov from the Kholmogorsk forests,

you'll enter Moscow." His voice boomed and his face grew even redder. "University! Young! Handsome! In medals and ribbons." And then he added quickly, like an aside, "I'll hang a wall of those spangles on you—we know what's what!"—and then moved back to the melodramatic declamation: "Step forward! Storm the walls of academe! But you'll be ambushed by those . . ."

The colonel opened his eyes and squinted in disgust.

"Those . . ."

He was looking for a word to substitute for "kikes," which was on the tip of his tongue, and which he had to force himself not to use around me.

"Those . . . rear rats," he said, relieved to find a substitute for "kikes." He went on in what he considered a Jewish accent.

" 'And vere are you goink?' they'll stop you. 'To study? And viz whose permission?' "

The iron was back in his voice. "You, of course, are bewildered. You try to explain yourself." He said that with pain and hurt. "Then I come forward. I push you aside gently. Allow me!" Now his voice is nothing but iron. "I take my pistol out of my pocket . . . and shoot. Fuck! Fuck! Fuck! Go on with your studies now!"

And he made a sweeping gesture inviting me to enter the university. Stepping over the bodies of the hindering Jews. So that I, also a Jew, but his son, could study without any problems.

I was orphaned twice. At the very beginning of the war, and at the very end. About two weeks before final victory, I buried my adoptive father, Colonel Galemba.

He didn't die in combat. He died after combat, when our regiment, having once again lost a good half of its men and almost all of its equipment, was sent behind the lines to regroup. It was in April, the end of April.

I don't know about other years, but in '45 the forests around Berlin were filled with cherry trees, white, thick, with a perfume so strong that it made your head ache. Throughout the woods, the sites of recent battles, lay scattered bodies. We picked up only our dead. The Germans decomposed among the mosses and ferns, in the damp shade of the cherry groves. The scent of decomposition, mixed with the smell of cherry blossoms, floated over the Brandenburg woods.

We found the elegant black lacquered carriage with tall, white-spoked wheels on the estate. The family crest of its owners was drawn in colorful detail on the black lacquer—two lions rampant.

Colonel Galemba liked the looks of the carriage. He decided to take a ride on the rustling paths through the woods, to the lakes that were loaded with fish, according to our men.

He took along the skeletal and regiment commissary as an assistant—Captain Kurylev was as meek and obedient as a trusty valet. Galemba, his jacket unbuttoned over his belly, fell back onto the seat, I got into the coach box, and Kurylev stood on the running board, which had room for only one foot. He rode the whole way on one foot, bending the other leg at the knee, which made him look like a stork.

Birds warbled in the forest, bees buzzed around the horse, and it seemed that there was no war in the world.

When we reached the lake I unhitched the horse, wound the reins around his shagging forelegs, and let him graze on the grassy lake shore. Reeds stuck up from the lake, with only one clear spot, where we set up the net. Colonel Galemba held one end. He had taken off his shoes and socks, tossed off his shirt, and remained in only his jodhpurs and purple undershirt. Captain Kurylev, stripped naked, went into the water with the other end. He wore only his green army cap with its black patent-leather visor to protect his bald head from the sun.

The captain, lifting his thin yellow feet high in the cold water, moved in and, urged by the colonel, dragged his end farther from shore, until he was chest deep.

"Now bring it in!" the colonel shouted loudly.

Galemba stood in one place, holding the net, while Kurylev dragged his end in a circle. Before he reached shore, he was completely engulfed by the water twice when he stepped into holes. The first time his cap floated off. When his seaweed-covered yellow scalp appeared, the colonel forbade him to go after the cap and ordered him to go on with the dragging. The cap floated on the ripples, and Captain Kurylev took a few more steps and went under again, but he did not let go of the net for fear of the colonel's wrath.

"Good man, Kurylev!" Galemba shouted from shore. "Good work!"

Poor Kurylev had made it to higher ground and, sputtering and teeth chattering, tried to answer the colonel.

"Glad to try, comrade colonel," he said glumly.

We didn't catch many fish: Galemba's shouts must have scared them away. The colonel grimaced and ordered the catch thrown back. I brought a tasseled German tablecloth from the carriage and spread it on the grass by the water. Kurylev brought a canister with alcohol and a few American canned goods. We drank and ate well and, completely drunk, barely managed to hitch the horse and head back. It was after noon by then, hot and stuffy. The fragrance of cherry blossoms was stronger, almost unbearable. The colonel was dozing, rocked by the comfortable seat. Kurylev, slowly warming up, swayed on one leg on the running board, and I tried to stay awake. The road was soon intersected by another, and that's where everything happened.

Down the perpendicular road came a raggedy line of Germans in gray-green dusty uniforms: armed, moving west. They were trying to turn themselves in to the Americans. There were many wandering groups like that around Berlin in those days. They avoided combat—they wanted to be in prison camps in the west.

They would have avoided us, but we came out in the intersection quite unexpectedly. The Germans scattered behind trees. One of them was too nervous and tossed a grenade under the wheels of our carriage.

The grenade exploded. A hot whirlwind passed along my back and head, knocking off my cap. The horse bolted and raced off. The wheels were whole—I could tell from the way the tires rustled on the gravel. I noticed out of the corner of my eye that the left board was empty: Captain Kurylev was gone. The colonel said nothing behind me.

We galloped into the estate, and I stopped the horse by the brown stacks of charcoal briquettes. I turned to the colonel. He sat, listing to one side with eyes shut, but his face was taking on a yellowish tinge. Then I saw a thin stream of blood along his stomach, coming through the purple undershirt. The colonel was mortally wounded, by a single shard. The carriage had not been damaged: not a single scratch.

The officers came running and sent a jeep for a doctor. They carried the colonel's body from the carriage and placed it on the stacks of charcoal, first covering them with the tablecloth we had used for our picnic. An orderly cut open the colonel's undershirt and bandaged his stomach to stop the bleeding.

I stood alone, to one side, by the unhitched horse and did not approach the crowd around the commander's body. I was a private, and they were all officers. They didn't like me very much. But as long as I was son of their commander, they carefully hid their hostility. Now that my protector was dying, I was a nobody. Army protocol rose between us.

One man remembered me: the dying man himself. Regaining consciousness for a moment, the colonel's murky gaze traveled around the officers bent over him, and I heard his hoarse, wheezing whisper: "Where's . . . my . . . youth in his prime?"

The officers beckoned to me. They stepped aside to

let me through to the charcoal stack where, lying on a velvet tablecloth as if it were a flag, my adoptive father was dying. I bent down to him and embraced him carefully, above the bandaged stomach. His eyes were sunken in dark shadows, but they were looking at my face. From the movement of his dried lips, which could not manage a smile, I saw that he recognized me.

I sobbed. My tears dropped on the bridge of his nose and he blinked his thick, shaggy eyelashes.

"It didn't work, son," he whispered.

"What?" I asked.

"I didn't make it to victory day. . . . Without me— you'll go to the university without me."

Even as he lay dying, this man who was basically a stranger to me could not give up his dream: to send his son to college.

"Study hard," he said. These were his last words. "Don't shame your father. . . ."

I covered my face with my hands, I was shouldered aside, and I heard the tense voice of the chief of staff. "It's over! He's gone."

I wept, my face against the wall, and a bony warm hand lay on my shoulder.

"Cry, boy. Tears wash the soul."

It was Samokhin.

I turned to him and pressed myself to him, scraping my face on his medals.

"Orphaned again," he muttered near my ear. "But you'll be fine. I'm still alive."

After Colonel Galemba's body had been brought into the house, a column of unarmed Germans entered the courtyard. Behind them limped their sole guard—tall and skinny Captain Kurylev, also unarmed. One of the prisoners had thrown the grenade that had killed my adoptive father. My red-rimmed eyes searched their dusty faces and I saw a killer in every one. But I couldn't force myself to feel hatred for any of them.

15

We were so crowded in the compartment of a passenger car that our faded shoulder boards bent and buckled, five soldiers to a seat, facing each other, toes touching. A large suitcase, a spoil of war, lay across our laps, its cardboard side now a table covered with newspaper. On it swayed two bottles of vodka, army-issue mugs with bent sides, thick uneven slices of bread and ham, and cans of pork sausage.

Men drank and laughed in every compartment of the endless train that raced merrily past ruined stations and rusted skeletons of burned cars. Conquered Germany lay outside the windows, with its pointy church spires; with gaping broken windows in little red box houses; with mountains of broken brick. And all was green with thick and juicy foliage, as if nature were trying to cover up the ruins left by war.

This was the first demobilization. Leaving Germany for Russia were the old men and the boys, all in faded uniforms with rows of ribbons and medals on their chests, American canned goods in their packs and German looted goods in German looted suitcases. In my car nine old soldiers and I.

We clinked mugs noisily, spilling the vodka. We dug our knives in the cans, pulling out dark pieces of American pork. Unwashed cucumbers crunched in our mouths. I sat next to Samokhin, pushed by his shoulder into the very corner of the compartment. I also sipped warm vodka from my mug, munching lazily and listening to what my elders were saying. They all talked at once, waving their arms, pushing each other in the chest, and leaning over the suitcase with wet lips to press a tearful kiss on another pair of wet lips as a sign of their eternal friendship to the grave.

The soldiers were excited by their return home, and they showed off pictures of their children. They shouted and sobbed, and every now and then they'd start up a drunken song.

In all the talk, one thing stood out: Germany, a bourgeois country, was so rich, and we Russians, even though we represented the state of peasants and workers, lived worse than cattle.

"Why, even their cattle live better than we do," a broad-chested sergeant with a flaxen mustache said angrily. "Have you seen the cowsheds? They have electricity, lights. And we burn kerosene in my house. My kids have never seen an electric light."

"You're lucky you have kerosene," another said. "Go try to get some. There's a shortage."

"Right," a third said. "We've never seen electricity in my village. We live like God's little birds—up with the sun and asleep with the sunset."

"And why is that?" Flaxen Mustache looked around sternly with watery, colorless eyes. "Their cows live it up in houses and we, Russian Orthodox Christians, grovel in cowsheds? What? You don't know?"

"You can't figure it out right away," Samokhin said, smoking a cigarette. "For instance, who here is a worker and who's a bourgeois? I haven't met a poor German. Every house has carpets, armchairs, chandeliers. . . . And the dishes? Does that mean that all of Germany is bourgeois? What's happened to the working class?"

"That means you haven't understood a thing." Flaxen Mustache sighed deeply. "Oh, my Slavic brothers! You haven't been beaten enough. . . . You haven't learned wisdom."

"Well, why don't you explain . . . if you're so smart," Samokhin said in a huff.

"Why, it's clear to a baby! What's the very first thing the Germans did? They write about it in the papers every day. Here's what they did. They did away with all the Jews. That's why they live like human beings."

"That's interesting," someone said. "It never occurred to me. But the sergeant is right."

"Wait till we get back to Russia," the sergeant went on. "We'll cleanse Russia of them. And then we'll start living no worse than the Germans, eh?"

With a heavy heart but with a pleasant smile I watched the soldiers nod in agreement. It didn't occur to anyone that I was the only Jew among them. Good old Samokhin, who knew, never gave it a second thought. For him I was who I was. The last thing he thought about was whether I was Jewish, Turkish, or something else.

In the meantime the sergeant with sun-bleached eyebrows and a short red nose peeling from sunburn got more heated.

"Brothers!" he called on the soldiers drunkenly. "We saved Russia from the Germans. . . . That's in the past. Now we have to save her from the Jews. . . . And then the Russian people can live and flourish.

"We don't count!" He struck his chest with a fist and the medals jangled. "We're old! We're manure! It's for young people to do. People like him!"

Everyone looked at me and in the drunken faces, in the dull, bleary eyes, I saw the conviction that I really was the man who would free Russia of Jews and make her flourish the way Hitler had made Germany flourish.

I tried feverishly to figure out what to do. Get up and kick the sergeant and start a free-for-all? Or simply spit in his overheated porcine face and get up with dignity and silently leave the compartment?

And here Samokhin spoke up. The poor old man was under the influence of the vodka and stuffiness. The fact that I, his favorite, was the center of attention of the whole compartment, and senior soldiers were looking at me kindly and with trust, delighted the old man. Not understanding what was what, flattered by their attitude toward me, he embraced me, pulled me by the neck to his prickly cheek, and moved the red, tobacco-stained tips of his mustache.

"He won't let you down! Believe me . . ."

That killed me. I pushed Samokhin away sharply. I got up, pushing the suitcase with vodka and the remains of the food from my lap, pulled my bag out from under the other things on the overhead rack, and left the compartment, shutting the door noisily.

The corridor was crowded with soldiers. A loud din came from the open compartments, while several looted accordions played different songs from different parts of the car. I pushed past the backs of soldiers staring out the windows, reached the baggage platform, clambered over it, and rested on the noisy platform between cars.

Germany raced backward to the right and left, the endless green trees flashing past along the asphalt road and the pointy roofs of burned houses. I wanted to cry. A childish hurt flooded my soul—and concentrated on Samokhin. His unwitting drunken treachery hurt most of all. He was a second father, after the death of Colonel Galemba. Rather, a third—the first was my real father, missing without a word, at the very start of the war.

I had no family in Russia. Samokhin was taking me home to his village near Penza, to be part of his large hungry family.

"What's the difference?" he had said when I tried to talk him out of it. "Where seven are hungry, there's room for an eighth. The village isn't like the city. The land will feed us. Mother Earth won't let us starve. We'll get a pig. Soon the cow will calve, there'll be milk. It's worse in the cities. You can't eat bricks."

And so we were on the way to his house, with two

free tickets to the Penza station and dry American rations for a week of travel.

I went along the next car, through the drunken chatter and accordion moans, and ended up in the next platform stuffed with looted things. I was getting away from Samokhin. I knew that he would come looking for me, not understanding what I ran away from.

And sure enough, soon at the other end of the car came Samokhin's anxious voice:

"Brothers! Have you seen a little soldier? Young, underage."

I crawled over the bags and accordion cases until I reached the ceiling and then crawled down the other side. I couldn't see Samokhin, but I could hear his tear-filled voice getting closer.

"A minor, brothers. We're traveling together to my village. . . . He's an orphan . . . doesn't have anyone else. Hey, brothers, hasn't anyone seen him?"

He was in the luggage platform muttering:

"This is terrible! God . . . I lost the boy . . . not in combat . . . not to a bullet . . . but on the road. . . . Help me, brothers. . . . How can I show up without him? I wrote in a letter he was coming. . . . They're expecting us both!"

I hid, holding my breath. I felt awfully sorry for the old man, but I didn't call out. I was too hurt.

Samokhin stood around, sighing and blowing his nose. And he left. When the train slowed down at the station, I jumped out of the car and ran to a neighboring freight train with the engine on the eastern end and climbed into an empty car. The passenger train I had been on ran past my eyes car by car and vanished. I never saw Samokhin again.

I was coming back to an empty Russia. I didn't have a family. I didn't even have pictures of my parents, and their faces were starting to blur in my memory.

But I remembered that in the city where my mother was born, my dead grandfather had had his own house, made of thick logs. The house was as sturdy as my grandfather—he built it with his own hands.

If it was still standing, then I was the only heir and owner of the house. I would sell it immediately. Prices were very high after the war, and with pocketfuls of money I would begin a new life.

Spurred on by these thoughts, I hurried to that city, which turned out to be heavily bombed, and then ran past the ruins and ashes, remembering where the house was.

Almost the entire street was demolished. No houses, no fences, only brick foundations, grown over with grass, the remains of charred logs and orphaned chimneys, remained. But our house was whole and unharmed, even the fence and the large gate with the same number it used to have before the war. I later learned that the house had not been burned down because German police had been stationed there.

I and the house had survived the war. I instantly became a person with a future.

I opened the gate.

I had no doubt that someone was living in the house. And as I walked to the house, I imagined with relish how I would stake my claim to the astonished residents and in a firm and not at all childish voice suggest that they get lost.

There were people in our house. And these people were standing in the yard and looking in bewilderment at the young soldier with a pack on his back standing at the gate.

Who was standing in the yard?

My mother. One. Just the way she was before the war, only very badly dressed. With a kerchief on her head, she was bent over a trough that billowed with white suds. She glanced at me, didn't recognize me, and went back to her wash.

My sister. Two. She had grown up over the years and had turned into a leggy teenager. I would never have recognized her if I hadn't seen her next to my mother. Naturally, she didn't recognize me either and simply looked at a young soldier with curiosity. In those days soldiers home from the front wandered around towns, seeking some kind of information about their loved ones.

My old Aunt Riva. Three. Lonely, childless, never married, she gave her heart to her numerous nephews and nieces, including me, whom she nursed and protected from parental wrath.

She was the one to recognize me.

Shading her eyes from the sun, she stared at me a long time and then said loudly and calmly, as if there were nothing amazing in what she said:

"I think that's . . ."

And she called me by the family diminutive that was used when I was very little.

I almost shouted, "Yes! It's me!"

But I said nothing. I couldn't say a word.

Then my mother looked up from the trough, squinted, straightened up and walked like a zombie toward me, wiping the soapsuds from her forearms. She walked stiffly, and her face was inexpressive.

I stood rooted to the spot and did not take a single step toward my mother. And she kept walking, recognizing me more with every step, and when she was very close, she opened her arms to embrace me. And here I committed an act for which any normal person would call me a bastard and a louse and would be absolutely correct. But Mama, my Mama, understood and didn't take offense.

I didn't let my mother embrace me. It would have been too much. I shouted, "As you were!"

And Mama's hands fell.

Then I offered her my hand and said simply, as if I had been gone a day:

"Hello, Mama."

She said nothing in reply and silently walked next to me to the house.

When all the excitement was over, Mother told me that at the height of the war, in a distant Siberian village, an old woman told her fortune with stones, she said that mother had lost two men and, as God was holy, both were alive. Mother said that the Siberian woman was right about one of us—I came back alive. But as for the other, she had made a mistake. Mama had the death notice.

Three weeks after my return, our gate opened and in walked my father. In a uniform like mine, with the same backpack.

And he was surprised, just like me, finding the whole family in the yard. You'll laugh, but he had come, just like me, to sell the house built by my grandfather. He had figured that the house might survive such a war, but not a Jewish family.

There's no point in dragging this out. My mother did not lose her mind. And I don't think she was even surprised.

"We are not like other people," she said.

Many many years later, when I was a highly successful adult, I gave my parents a present: a trip for two to a privileged government sanitarium. In all her life Mother had never been to a resort. Like a workhorse she carried the full weight of the family pack on her back: bringing up children without nannies or grandmas, having to re-create a family hearth in a new place almost every year, in strange apartments and army barracks. And the division was always sent to the sticks, suitable for strategic purposes but not for comfortable living.

In those days there were no washing machines, no refrigerators, and only wood-burning stoves. All the heavy work fell on the uncomplaining women. Once my mother said that the state was unfair in giving medals and ribbons to the officers. Officers' wives, who were doomed to a nomadic gypsy life, had more right to those awards.

Mother lived through war and evacuation, and spent time as a widow. And she labored and labored, without straightening her back, without a day of rest.

And then in her sunset years came the opportunity for a real rest. A whole month of carefree leisure in luxurious surroundings, under the strict supervision of doctors and nurses, maids and waiters. The sanitarium where I took my parents was not open to ordinary folk. The country's elite went there. In a deep forest, on the banks of a lake, the sanitarium resembled a castle. My parents were given a suite with a balcony overlooking the pines that faced east and west, so as to stay with the sun from sunrise to sunset. Everything shone and sparkled here, every wish was anticipated and immediately gratified by the throng of servants.

About two weeks later, while on a business trip in the area, I made time and went to visit them.

First I saw my father, strolling under the pines wearing a white panama hat. A terry-cloth towel stuck out of his sports bag. He was coming back from the beach.

"Where's Mama?" I asked.

Father's face darkened. He did not reply. He merely nodded over toward the main building.

"Is she sick?"

"You'll see."

I was worried. Father didn't say another word as the sparkling elevator carried us upstairs and while we walked along the thick silent carpets of the glass-enclosed terrace. Father stopped at their suite, looked at me sadly, and flung open the door, nodding for me to come in.

In the living room all the furniture had been pushed over to the walls, chairs set up on the tables, and the carpets rolled back. The painted wooden floors were wet, and in the far corners, skirts hitched up, knelt my mother, washing the floor with a rag. Wearing an old worn dress suitable for housework, she was so engrossed in her work that she didn't notice us at first.

When Mother finally saw me, she gave me a guilty look.

"Well, I'm not used to being served," she said. "The woman cleaning our floor is older than me. How can I let her clean up after me? I can handle it myself. At least I have something to do. . . . You can go crazy just doing nothing."

She quickly went into the bedroom to change, and Father and I stood in the doorway of the living room, where the wet floor gave off a cozy and fresh homey smell.

"Well, what do you say?" Father said, and gave me a sad look.

I grinned from ear to ear.

"We're very lucky, Father. We are *not* like other people."